SILENT STAR

SILENT STAR

Hope was fragile

that long-ago winter

in Haven, Pennsylvania.

TRACIE
PETERSON

BETHANYHOUSE
MINNEAPOLIS, MINNESOTA 55438

Silent Star
Copyright © 2003
Tracie Peterson

Cover design by Koechel Peterson & Associates

Unless otherwise identified, Scripture quotations are from the
King James Version of the Bible.

Published by Bethany House Publishers
11400 Hampshire Avenue South
Bloomington, Minnesota 55438

Bethany House Publishers is a Division of
Baker Book House Company, Grand Rapids, Michigan.

Printed in the United States of America

Library of Congress Cataloging-in-Publication Data

Peterson, Tracie.
   Silent Star / by Tracie Peterson.
     p.   cm.
   ISBN 0-7642-2824-2 (pbk.)
   1. World War, 1939-1945—Pennsylvania—Fiction. 2. World
War, 1939-1945—Casualties—Fiction. 3. Telegraph—
Employees—Fiction. 4. Pennsylvania—Fiction. 5. Aged
women—Fiction. 6. Grief—Fiction. I. Title.

PS3566.E7717S56   2003
813'.54—dc22   2003014246

Books by Tracie Peterson

www.traciepeterson.com

Controlling Interests
The Long-Awaited Child
Silent Star
A Slender Thread • *Tidings of Peace*

BELLS OF LOWELL*
Daughter of the Loom • *A Fragile Design*
These Tangled Threads

DESERT ROSES
Shadows of the Canyon • *Across the Years*
Beneath a Harvest Sky

WESTWARD CHRONICLES
A Shelter of Hope • *Hidden in a Whisper*
A Veiled Reflection

RIBBONS OF STEEL†
Distant Dreams • *A Hope Beyond*
A Promise for Tomorrow

RIBBONS WEST†
Westward the Dream • *Separate Roads*
Ties That Bind

SHANNON SAGA‡
City of Angels • *Angels Flight*
Angel of Mercy

YUKON QUEST
Treasures of the North • *Ashes and Ice*
Rivers of Gold

NONFICTION
The Eyes of the Heart

*with Judith Miller   †Judith Pella   ‡with James Scott Bell

To all those who serve
and have served to keep our country free.
And to those who wait behind at home
for their loves ones to return.
Thank you for your sacrifice.

TRACIE PETERSON is a popular speaker and bestselling author who has written over fifty books, both historical and contemporary fiction. Tracie and her family make their home in Montana.

Visit Tracie's Web site at:
www.traciepeterson.com.

CHAPTER ONE

*S*NOW FELL in gentle swirls on the streets of Haven, Pennsylvania, as the laughter of children at play echoed on the breeze. Christmas would arrive in a few weeks—weeks of expectation and school programs, weeks of blistering cold and winter pageantry. Anticipation mounted with each passing day, each snow-flake.

For the moment—this one small moment—Andy Gilbert found he could forget about his troubles, forget about the war that raged across the world. The chilling bite of the air invigorated him, and the scent of wood-smoke and pine awakened happy memories of his childhood days.

He longed to preserve moments like these in time like a perfect apple picked and canned at just the exact second its sweetest flavor could be had. Gazing about, Andy could think of no other place he'd rather live. His mother had often said Haven was God's kiss upon Pennsylvania. She'd lived there since her birth, had raised her only child and buried her husband there. She'd wanted nothing more out of life than what Haven had to offer.

Andy had felt much the same. He under-stood his mother's love of the town, for in the midst of thousands of people, the quiet community reached out to one another like a large extended family. Mrs. Butler shared baby clothes with Mrs. Lambert, and Mrs. Davis traded pickle recipes with Mrs. Masters. The men who frequented Davis's Barbershop said there was no better group of folks in the whole world than those who lived right there in Haven.

Andy agreed. But times had changed, and the people of Haven had changed with it. At least, they had when it came to him.

"Margaret, come here at once and help me carry these packages," a woman's shrill voice sounded. Andy looked up and saw Mrs. Parrish and her daughter Margaret. The woman caught sight of Andy and quickly looked away. Taking hold of her daughter's arm, she appeared to bolster herself as Andy walked by. Neither woman would acknowledge him.

Saying nothing, just as he knew she would

prefer, Andy limped along the snowy sidewalk. He hunkered into the warmth of his father's hand-me-down coat. It was hard to believe Pop had been dead for three years now. The same car accident that had left Andy's left foot lame had taken the life of his father. Andy tried hard to not think about it, just as he used to try hard not to limp. Especially around his mother.

His mother had off-handedly told him once that his limp was like a constant reminder of the accident and her loss. To Andy, the limp didn't conjure up memories of his loss. Those memories were with him daily . . . nightly . . . always. A dull ache haunted his every waking moment. He even dreamed of the pain, only to awaken to the reality of it.

He walked a little slower, nearly dragging his foot now. The end of the day was always the worst, and cold weather made the pain even more pronounced. The doctor had once said to him, "Andy, you'll never walk without pain, but at least you're alive. That's something to be glad about."

At first Andy had agreed and seen the blessing of it. At first.

Then his mother had sat him down to explain that with his father dead, there was no income—no hope of paying the mortgage or the coal bill. So Andy quit school at age fifteen in order to go to work at the only job he could find. The telegraph company was run by his father's best friend, John Ross. John too had suffered a terrible loss at the death of Andy's father. When he heard that Andy was looking for work, John made the decision to take a chance on the crippled boy.

"I owe it to your father to give you a chance," John Ross had told him. *"Don't let either one of us down."*

Andy, ever eager to please, had quickly

proven that he had the energy and spirit to get the job done. He'd been at work only two months, however, when the Japanese bombed Pearl Harbor and the world turned upside down.

The 28th Infantry Division, a National Guard Unit from Pennsylvania, had been called into service the previous February for one year of active duty. Now those men, many of whom Andy knew personally, were caught up in a world war, answering the call for citizen soldiers. Day after day, month after month, and year after year, Andy had watched the government telegrams come in. They came in following the ebb and flow of battles across the Pacific and European Theaters. He'd seen the names of people who were dear friends, knowing the news would be heartbreaking.

Now, three years later, Andy wished he'd never agreed to deliver telegrams—never walked through John Ross's door. The money might have kept them from losing the house, but the price of this job had cost him his heart—his soul.

The wind picked up and blew hard against him. Ahead on the snowy walk, Andy spotted Mr. and Mrs. Harrison from over on Fourth Street. They'd lost two boys to the war. Joseph, who was a year older than Andy, had been aboard the *Arizona* when the Japanese had sent it to the bottom of Pearl Harbor. Matthew, two years Joseph's senior, had disappeared somewhere over France when the bomber on which he held the tail-gunner position had been blown up by enemy fire. There was no body to confirm the death, but there was also no hope of survivors.

Andy watched the Harrisons as they caught sight of him. They moved quickly and quietly to the opposite side of the street. There was no holiday wave or friendly greeting. They walked on, heads down, holding on to each other as if Andy had some power to pull them apart—or to steal their next son in line, Bobby, who served with the 28th.

Unshed tears welled in Andy's eyes and crusted as ice on his lashes. Every day it was the same. Every day people looked the other way when Andy came into their midst. War news was never good news. Even in victorious battles for the Americans and their allies there was always a long list of wounded and dead. Telegrams were sent out daily to inform people of the death of their sons and husbands and fathers. Andy was the bearer of bad tidings— the Grim Reaper of Haven, Pennsylvania. No one could bear to talk to him or even look at him for more than a passing glance. To offer more might well invite his attention, and that in turn might bring the news of death.

To people who only years earlier had called him friend, he was dreaded as surely as sickness and war. He was the unspeakable fear that walked the streets of their town. They wished him obliterated as surely as they wished an end to the war.

Andy struggled to force the negative thoughts from his mind, but nothing in his life could inspire him to take on the spirit of the coming holidays. Thanksgiving would soon be celebrated, but Andy felt no thanks.

He fingered the hole in his pocket, the tattered edges catching against his torn gloves. He wondered how a person might go about sewing such a thing. His mother could have done the job, but she was gone now—"passed on to glory," as the pastor had told him at her grave. She'd gone and left Andy completely alone without the knowledge of how to do a great many things. Important things. Necessary things.

Cooking was a complete mystery to him. Andy still couldn't do much more than open a can of beans and heat them on the stove. He would often look at the little collection of spices his mother had owned and contemplate what she must have done with such things. The same was true of flour and soda, vinegar and cornstarch. How were such things put together to create edible concoctions?

Andy crossed Main Street at Ninth and made his way another two blocks to the house on Chester Street that he called home. He'd made the last payment on the house two weeks before his mother's death. The place belonged to him now, free and clear. Yet somehow it didn't offer him near the comfort he'd thought it would.

Darkness greeted him as Andy opened the back door. A rush of stale air only marginally warmer than the air outside hit him as he walked into the house. Shivering, he turned on the lights and immediately went downstairs to the coal bin. There wasn't much left. He'd have to remember to order his coal rations. He picked up the scuttle and quickly scraped up the last of the coal. Taking it upstairs, Andy thought of how his mother would have had supper waiting for him, the house toasty warm. She would have asked him how his day went and commiserated with him on the sorrow he'd had to deliver.

Pausing for a moment to look at the empty chair where she would have sat to share supper with him, Andy mourned her loss all over again. The doctor said it was a cancer—probably something she'd carried around inside her for a long, long time. She'd faded away, right before his very eyes, until suddenly she was no longer there at all.

"These things can't be helped," the doctor told Andy. *"We just don't know much about sickness like this. We don't know how to treat it— to cure it. All we can do is make her comfortable."*

But they hadn't even accomplished that.

Andy's mother had died in pain, praying for an end so that she could go home to be with her husband.

Shaking off the memory, Andy fed the stove and worked to get a fire going. If he did it just right, the fire would last well into the night and keep him warm until morning. The secret was to use just the right amount of coal—not too much at a time, but not too little either. He'd learned quickly that there was a real knack for such things.

It wasn't until an hour later that Andy finally took off his coat and changed out of his uniform. He inspected the outfit for stains, gave it a quick sniff, and decided it was good enough to wear at least another day. He hung the shirt up and draped the trousers across the ladder-back chair in his bedroom before pulling on his flannel shirt and a pair of old wool trousers that had belonged to his father. Stepping from his room, the last thing he did was to take up a well-worn sweater from the back of the door. The house would never be so warm that he wouldn't need that added layer.

Andy put water on to boil and put an egg in the pan. He remembered seeing his mother do this on more than one occasion, but he never knew exactly how long to keep the egg in the water. He was too ashamed to ask his mother's good friend Harriet, so he generally let the egg boil for at least half an hour. It always seemed to be done by then—a little rubbery, but nevertheless edible. He'd thought about cutting back on the time, but fear of the unknown kept him fixed at the thirty-minute mark.

While the egg boiled, he sliced the last of the bread. Arranging it in a pan, he toasted it atop the stove. His stomach rumbled loudly as the aroma touched his senses. Leaving the slices browning, he poured himself a glass of milk and drank half of it before heading back to turn the toast. It was the last of the milk, the last of the bread. Pretty much the last of everything.

He was resolved not to feel sorry for himself, but his willpower was also running in short supply. With his meal finally ready to eat, Andy sat down to the kitchen table and switched on the radio. A soft, velvetlike melody spilled into the room, offering a soothing background for his meal. Andy thought about praying but decided otherwise, just as he had every other night since his mother's death. Why bother? God wasn't listening.

The house seemed huge and so very silent as Andy ate his supper. He thought of how small he'd thought the house only three or four years ago. He remembered asking his dad why they couldn't move so that he could have a big bedroom like his friend Ray. His father had laughed, saying most boys his age would have just been glad to have a room of their own—some would have even coveted a bed of their own. Andy knew that was true enough. He remembered when the Harrison boys had slept three to a bed. It was one of the reasons Matthew went into the service. He'd joked that he could finally have his own bunk. And now he was gone.

When he finished his meager meal, Andy quietly washed the dishes, rinsed out the milk bottle, and then checked the stove one last time. He switched off the kitchen light and walked through the pitch-blackness to his bedroom just down the hall. The utter silence of the house held him captive, and he paused for a moment and closed his eyes against the darkness. It was like being entombed alive. The darkness . . . the stillness . . . the cold.

Minutes later he lay in his bed, the same darkness and silence as his companions. He thought of his mother and father. They'd worked all of their lives to make this house a home. To make it their own. Now they were gone, leaving Andy and the house as awkward companions.

"I miss them so much," he whispered, breaking the stillness.

He might have borne their absence easier had he friends who rallied round to ensure that he not grow too lonely. But most of his boyhood friends had gone to fight. It was the patriotic thing to do, after all. But Andy's classification was 4-F, thanks to his unpatriotic lame foot. And because of his job and the gloom that seemed to surround him, even the families he'd known all of his life wanted very little to do with him.

He was reminded of an event that had happened only two days earlier when he'd passed by a mother and her two children. He'd been walking to work, the snow making it impossible to bicycle. When the woman noticed him, she quickly grabbed her children by the hand and pulled them close, almost as if Andy could take their lives in a glance. He'd heard the smaller child ask his mother if Andy was the boogeyman. He hadn't heard her reply, but the look in her eyes as he'd passed by made her thoughts clear.

He was the boogeyman.

⁂ ⁂ ⁂

The next day Andy awoke to a frosty chill, the temperature suggesting the fire had most likely gone out early in the night. He snuggled down into the quilts, having no reason to hurry his rising. There was no more coal, so until the delivery truck could bring it around, Andy would just have to bundle up and make do. Staying in bed a little longer than usual was far too tempting on this cold morning.

Sundays were always hard and this Sunday was no exception. When his mother had been alive the routine had been simple: They would attend church services together at the Eleventh Street Methodist Church and then come home to enjoy a quiet day. Then she'd gotten sick, and with each passing week her frailty had increased with the pain.

After a month, maybe two, she'd been unable to get out of bed to go anywhere. When that happened, Andy had stopped going to church, choosing instead to sit by her side throughout most of the day. The pastor, a young man named Bailey who seemed ill at ease with sickness, had come to visit on many occasions, but he was never any comfort, and Andy finally suggested he not return. He hadn't seen Bailey again until the funeral.

Andy's mother hadn't even realized that the man had stopped coming. Her days blended one into the other as the doctor strived to keep ahead of her pain with his limited variety of medications.

With his mother gone, Sunday seemed strange . . . almost foreign. It was good to have the day to himself, but there was also an awkwardness about it. He liked to read the newspaper and see what was happening in the war, but at the same time he dreaded it. There were a few books in the house, but Andy had reread those so many times he knew them practically by heart. During the summer he toyed with a small garden in the backyard. His own little victory garden, he called it. He was a poor farmer, however. He'd managed nothing more than a few potatoes and onions and a handful of very scrawny beets.

So spending his time was often a simple matter of listening to the radio and napping. He'd grown old before his time—weary from the weight of responsibility and no one with whom to share it.

Yawning and stretching as best he could under the covers, Andy forced himself to sit up. For the first time in a long month of Sundays, he actually had a purpose.

He decided to forego trying to figure out anything for breakfast. Instead, he dressed warmly and took up a saw that hung in the mudroom. In his backyard, a large pine tree offered shade in the summer and the hope of springtime green in the winter.

Carefully, Andy trimmed branches from the pine. He only needed a few. Gathering the pieces in his arms, Andy took them to the kitchen table. For the rest of the morning he worked to fashion a wreath for his mother and father's grave. The project gave him a feeling of accomplishment and passed the time in a bearable way.

Outside and across the alley, Andy heard the laughter of the neighborhood children at play. A quick glance at his watch showed the hour to be after one. Church was out and lunch was over. No doubt the kids were building forts and snowmen. They would probably play all afternoon. Andy envied their happiness—their ability to keep thoughts of war from overshadowing the beauty around them.

As he walked through the neighborhoods toward the cemetery, Andy could see the bustle of activities going on in the houses that he passed. Families were gathered for a day of rest—making plans for Thanksgiving and Christmas, enjoying their time together.

He found it hard to keep walking, knowing that he had no part in the warmth and love that could be seen there. He wished they would all just pull the drapes and close the shutters. *It's better not to even look*, he told himself. *It's less painful not knowing what's happening than to watch and know that I have no place.*

But even when the drapes were pulled there was the stark, unforgettable reminder of the blue and gold stars that represented those in the service. Blue for the living. Gold for the dead. Banners of recognition and pride. Banners of hope . . . and of sorrow.

Andy knew a sort of fatal attraction to those silent stars. He watched for them—searching the windows of each house where he delivered those horrible little telegrams. He felt personally responsible for every gold star he saw that day on Chester Street, Washington Street, and all the others across the town.

No wonder the residents of those houses hated the very sight of him. It was no different from when the Williams family, who lived across the street, had lost their three-year-old son to meningitis. Mr. Williams finally took down the swing where the boy had played, for the sight of it was too painful. Just as the sight of Andy was too painful. If they could remove him, Andy had no doubt they would do exactly that.

The walk to the cemetery gave Andy plenty of time to consider his plight. He often thought of running away. After all, there were others who delivered telegrams, just as he did. There were other telegraph stations across the nation where other lonely 4-Fs worked to keep the lines of communication open. Someone would keep spreading the message if he decided to walk away. Someone would continue to bear the bad news. Why should it be him?

But then he remembered how hard his father had worked to buy the house. *"This will be yours one day, Andy,"* his father had told him with great pride.

And now it was his. His alone. Bought and paid for. How could he just walk away from it? Sell it and leave for another part of the country? He'd only find other mothers and wives who were dreading those horrible slips of paper just as much as they dreaded them in Haven, Pennsylvania.

Andy opened the wrought-iron gate to the cemetery and shuffled through the snow. The uncleared path surprised him. The caretaker was usually quite good about tending the walkways. When he drew near to the place where his parents' graves lay side by side, Andy cut across the field and came to stand directly at the head of their resting place.

He cleared away the snow from his parents' simple headstones. He gently traced the letters of each name.

H-E-R-M-A-N G-I-L-B-E-R-T
V-E-R-N-A G-I-L-B-E-R-T

Placing the wreath between them, Andy spoke softly. "The war is still on. Our boys from the 28th have the proud distinction of being some of the first Americans in Nazi Germany. They're fighting hard and no doubt they'll be dying hard too." He paused momentarily to adjust the piece of ribbon he'd tied to the greenery.

"I'll be delivering a lot of those telegrams," he continued. "I'd just as soon not do it. But, Pop, you always said to see a job through to the finish. I don't know when this war will end, but I'm trying hard to see it through and make you proud."

Somehow just talking to his parents like this helped Andy. He could almost imagine them sitting there listening, nodding and sympathizing.

"The president tells us to keep our spirits up, but to be truthful, I'm having a real hard time with it. With both of you gone, I'm just not sure why it matters anymore."

"Excuse me."

Andy looked over his shoulder, stunned to find an elderly woman standing directly behind him. He jumped up and stared at her, openmouthed. She smiled sweetly.

"I couldn't help but notice you here. There's no one else," she said, waving her arm at the expanse of the small cemetery.

Andy looked away, almost frightened by the woman's pleasant voice and winning smile. She obviously didn't know who he was. Of course, he wasn't wearing his uniform and there was always the possibility that she was new to the area.

"I'm sorry if I startled you," she continued. "My name is Estella. Estella Nelson."

Andy looked up, still not sure what to say. Estella smiled and adjusted her scarf. "And you are?"

Andy felt his mouth go dry. "Ah . . . I'm . . . ah . . . Andy. Andy Gilbert." He couldn't be sure, but he thought his voice cracked as if he were thirteen all over again.

"Andy, it's a pleasure to meet you. Who were you visiting just now?"

He shifted uneasily, his feet growing colder by the minute. "My parents."

"I see," she said, glancing past him to the stones. "You seem so young to be without them."

Andy nodded. He could think of nothing to say in reply. Thoughts flooded his mind, overwhelming him with questions, but words failed to form on his lips.

"I was visiting my husband's grave. He's been gone ten years now," Estella told him. "Some days it seems as though he left me only yesterday, and other times it feels like he's been gone for a hundred years." She smiled sweetly at him. "Is that how it feels for you—with them?"

Andy still didn't know what to say. This type of conversation was awkward and startling all at the same time. Even his mother's dear friends had very little to say to him when they met him in the ration lines or at the bank. Harriet, in fact, had moved away just last week to live with her daughter in Milwaukee. She promised to write and keep in touch with Andy, but he doubted she would. That left just Miriam, and she had a house on the other side of town. It was not only inconvenient to go visiting, but the cold weather made it downright dangerous.

"I'm sorry if I've intruded," Estella said softly. "It's just that I've only been back to Haven for about three months. I lived in Pittsburgh for almost ten years with my mother after Howard died. When she passed on a few months back, I came back here to the house Howard worked so hard for." She looked around and smiled. "I thought perhaps you were in need of company as much as I am."

Andy shook his head. "You wouldn't want my company if you knew who I was."

She chuckled. "Sounds intriguing."

"No," Andy whispered. "It's not intriguing at all. Just painful."

CHAPTER TWO

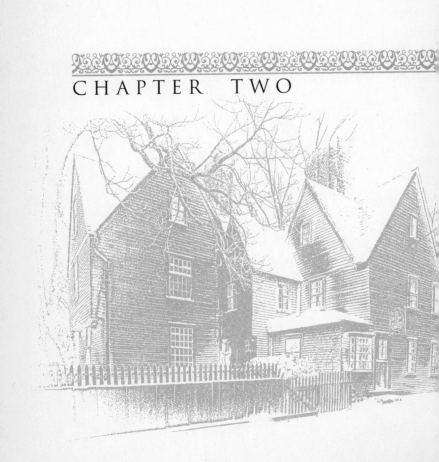

ESTELLA SAW the anguish in the boy's eyes. He was such a sweet-looking fella, red hair peeking out from beneath an overly large fedora. The hat had probably belonged to his father. A memento, she thought, of a man whose role the young boy hoped to fill.

"I find that misery is eased when it's shared

with another," she offered.

Andy shook his head. "Not this misery." He walked back toward the gate and Estella knew what she had to do.

"Wait, please," she called. Following him to the street, she smiled again. "It's terribly cold out here. Why don't you come home with me and have something hot to drink? I have plenty of coffee." She watched the emotion play on Andy's face. He seemed to want her company, but at the same time there was something about him that appeared uncomfortable in her presence.

"I can't," Andy finally answered. He pushed his gloved hands down into his coat pockets and began walking away.

"But it's Sunday. Surely there's nothing too pressing that can't wait until later," she added, hurrying to catch up with him.

Andy stopped and stared at her for a moment. "You don't understand."

Estella reached out and gently touched his arm. "Maybe not, but I'd like to."

He looked to the ground. "No. This isn't the kind of thing you'd ever understand. No one does."

"Try me. It hardly seems fair to judge me by the standards of other people."

"Fine," he said sternly. "Just remember, you are the one who forced this. Obviously you don't know me or what I do."

"So tell me." Estella had always been a woman who dealt with life matter-of-factly. Her husband said it was her Italian background, but she doubted it; she always figured it to be her own nosiness.

Andy struggled for several silent moments before he finally blurted out, "I deliver telegrams."

She frowned. It made little sense. She'd figured with the weight of guilt—or whatever emotion it was—that wore this boy down that at the very least he was some kind of confidence man. "I thought maybe you were a bank robber or a murderer," she said in a joking tone. "Delivering telegrams is nothing to be ashamed of."

"I might as well be a murderer. I bring the news of death and people hate me for it. You have no idea how they avoid me. You couldn't understand or you would never have approached me."

"Is that what this is all about?" Estella questioned.

"Isn't it enough?"

Estella stamped her feet to warm them a bit. "I hardly think so. So you are the bearer of bad tidings. Someone has to do it. Surely you aren't the only telegram delivery boy in town. How do the others feel?"

"I wouldn't know," Andy replied curtly. "I've never asked them."

"Hmm." Estella nodded. "Then it's

probably fair to guess that they've never asked you either."

"Of course they haven't."

She nodded again. "Then that would explain it."

Andy's frustration was apparent. "Explain what?"

"The fact that you feel so alone—so awkward in trying to explain this situation to me now."

"Look, it doesn't matter. People fear me, turn away from me because I bring them the news that their child or husband is dead. They want nothing to do with me and neither should you." He turned to walk away, and Estella let him proceed several paces before calling out to him.

"I have some cream—it's not much, but it would be enough for coffee."

Andy stopped in his tracks and turned.

"Why?" The depth of his anguish rang out in that one word.

"Why what? I offer you coffee and you ask why? Because I'm a lonely old lady and I like redheaded boys." She grinned. "Do you need more of a reason?"

He never even cracked a smile, and Estella's heart went out to him. Poor miserable child. So full of pain and sorrow, so unloved and forgotten. *God, I see now why you sent me out here on this cold day. This poor boy is dying from loneliness and the wounds others have inflicted on him.*

"Look, Andy Gilbert, you needn't turn down perfectly good coffee and cream just because some people have made you feel unwelcome. They'll get over it and so will you. You aren't the reason their children are dead and they know this only too well. They are in pain, Andy, and people in pain often do not understand the wounds they give others. They lash out, cutting and maiming, mindless of their actions because they are blinded by the anguish that fills their souls. You mustn't judge them too harshly."

"They've judged me harshly . . . and falsely," Andy murmured.

She smiled. "It happened to our Lord as well."

Andy shook his head. "I don't want to talk about God. It's His fault that all this is happening to begin with." He met her face, his expression hard. "I don't want any part of talking to God."

"I never said you had to talk to God, Andy."

He appeared confused. "But you said . . ."

"I said they judged Jesus harshly and falsely. I was merely pointing out that you aren't alone."

"That's where you're wrong, Mrs. Nelson.

I'm very much alone . . . and I intend to stay that way."

This time she let him go. She watched him limp down the road, his left foot dragging along in the snow. *Oh, the pain he suffers is so great, Father,* she prayed. *I could feel it just standing across from him. I could see it in his eyes and hear it in his voice. He's slipping away from life, Lord. He needs your help. Maybe even my help.* She moved down the street toward her own little bungalow, a plan formulating in her mind.

⁂ ⁂ ⁂

Andy thought of the old woman the next day as he stood in line for his groceries. He couldn't express how much it had meant to him that she would stand there and talk to him even after knowing about his job and the way other people felt about him. He had wanted so much to go with her—to share her coffee and cream. He could almost taste it even now.

Andy didn't recognize any of the people in line with him. He'd gone to a grocer on the other side of town where he wasn't as well known. He'd kept his father's coat tightly buttoned and hoped no one would notice his uniform pants. No one spoke to him much, but neither did they turn away from him. He blended rather obscurely into the crowd.

"Did you hear the news?" one man asked the woman in front of Andy. "They say our boys in the 28th are stompin' those Germans all the way back to Berlin. Let Hitler deal with *that*."

The woman smiled and answered in animated excitement, "I know, I know. My sister telephoned to tell me. Maybe the war will be over by Christmas. Wouldn't that be marvelous?"

The man nodded and stepped up to pay for his purchases. As with every other customer, the man had to present his ration book and identification. Finally the cashier tore out his coupons and told him how much he owed her. The procedure was repeated for the woman, and finally it was Andy's turn.

"You're saving your cans for the war effort, right?" the cashier asked as she sacked several cans of beans. She was a cheerful sort with a heart full of enthusiasm.

Andy nodded but said nothing. He gave the woman a weak smile.

"There's just so much we can do to help, you know. The ladies at my church are having a scrap drive. We have a box here in the store, so if you come back before the twentieth of this month be sure and bring any fabric you don't need or old rags. Oh, and the Girl Scouts are having a clothing drive. There's a box for that too."

"I'll see what I can do," Andy said, showing her his identification and offering his money.

With sacks in hand, Andy walked back home. The store windows had cheerful displays, proof that owners were trying their best to rally everyone's spirits. Amidst the routine accouterments declaring sales on various products there were also the ever-present signs of a country at war. A poster embracing the spirit of Christmas declared, "The Present With a Future—WAR BONDS" as a jolly Santa sprinkled war bonds down on the holiday houses below his sleigh.

Since the house was paid for, Andy had used some of his extra money to purchase some bonds. He knew it was his patriotic duty, but more than this, he felt it was almost an atoning. He couldn't be with his buddies fighting in the 28th, but he could help support them from afar.

Knowing he still needed toothpaste, Andy crossed the street to the five-and-dime, finding the store surprisingly busy with customers. He edged his way through the crowd, quickly locating what he'd come for. He juggled the sacks to free his hand.

"Andy Gilbert!"

He looked up to find a young woman, long blond hair streaming. "Don't you remember me? It's Mary Beth Iseman. I was a year behind you in school."

Andy nodded, feeling very shy. "Yeah, I remember you."

"Well, I haven't seen you in a long time. We moved into town from the country. We're even going to a new church and everything. Poppy said we couldn't make the long drive to our old church since he needs to conserve gas and tires for work. So here we are." She barely paused to draw a breath. "Did you know that Sammy is in Europe with the 28th? They're doing very well. We had a letter . . . well, actually Sammy's wife, Kay, had a letter just the other day. She lives with us, you know."

"No, I don't suppose I did," Andy said, still completely taken aback by her chatterbox conversation.

She tucked a strand of hair behind her ear and continued. "Sammy says everything is going really well. We don't know exactly where he is, but he's always trying to tell Kay with little coded words. They agreed before he left that certain words would be for some of the countries and such." She lowered her voice. "I don't suppose I should have said that. Just don't tell anyone. Mama says it might cause problems—loose lips and all, don'tcha know."

Andy looked around, feeling like someone was watching him. He spied Mrs. Iseman. She looked the same as he remembered from his school days. Sometimes Mrs. Iseman had

actually come to substitute for some of the
teachers. She'd always had a smile and kind
word for everyone, but today she was reserved.
Speaking in hushed covered-mouth whispers
to the barber's wife, Mrs. Davis, Mrs. Iseman
nodded, all the while watching Andy. A sense
of dread washed over him as the woman finally
made her way toward them.

"Mary Beth, what do you think you're
doing?" her mother questioned, coming upon
them. Andy cringed at the tone in her voice.

"Mama, this is Andy Gilbert. I went to
school with him."

"Yes, I *know* who he is." Her words took on
a deeper meaning for Andy.

"Can we invite him home for supper?"
Mary Beth asked her mother. "I want to tell
him all about Sammy and show him the letters."

"I'm sorry," Mrs. Iseman said in a stilted

tone. "I . . . well . . . it isn't convenient to invite him tonight."

"But, Mama . . ."

"Excuse me," Andy said, pushing past the two women, "I need to be going. I have other plans."

He then exchanged his old empty tube for the new tube of toothpaste and paid for the purchase. He hurried from the store, not even bothering to bid good-bye to Mary Beth. Her gentle voice and sweet smile had brightened an otherwise dreary day. How long had it been since he'd seen her and talked to her? At least three years.

The Isemans had lived on a farm just at the edge of town. It had been in the family for many generations, with Mary Beth's father and uncle helping their father run the place. Mary Beth's father, however, had taken an interest in running a freight service and gradually left the farm to his father and brother. After the passing of Mary Beth's grandfather, Andy recalled there had been some concern that the farm would be sold to pay debts. The brothers, however, had rallied and managed to hang on to the place. Andy thought it sad that Mr. Iseman should find it necessary now to leave and move into town. He was no doubt freighting things for the government and military now, as the cost would probably be too prohibitive for civilians.

At home, Andy was relieved to find that the coal delivery had come. They'd dumped the load through the basement chute, just as arranged. Taking a bucket load upstairs, Andy got the stove fired up and waited while the warmth spread across the room. He was more tired than he could remember ever being. He even contemplated forgoing supper, but the rumbling of his stomach finally won out over the soreness of his feet and back.

He opened a can of beans and while they

heated, Andy made a small pot of coffee. The aroma reminded him again of the old woman he'd met at the cemetery. Mrs. Nelson. Estella Nelson. He almost smiled as he thought of her. She had been so very persistent—tempting him with cream, not caring about his job duties. For just a moment he tried to imagine what it might have been like to share her hospitality.

Spreading his mother's well-worn red gingham cloth across the kitchen table, Andy couldn't help but think of Mary Beth Iseman as well. She looked nothing like the scrawny girl he remembered. She had grown up and she was quite pretty, but it was her spirit that attracted him most—the joy in her expression and the delight and excitement in her voice.

Andy let the memory of their meeting wash over him again and again. How could she be so happy in the middle of a war? How could she be happy, not knowing what tomorrow might bring?

Setting the table with the beans, coffee, and a few crackers, Andy continued to think of Mary Beth. She'd wanted to have him over for supper. She hadn't understood her mother's negative reply. It was clear Mrs. Iseman had wanted to think up some excuse for why it wouldn't work for Andy to join them. She would probably tell her daughter that he would only bring a curse upon their household, or perhaps she would comment that Andy's lowly station in life was no match for Mary Beth. Whatever she came up with, it didn't matter.

As much as he would have loved to share supper with anyone, Andy knew he would only hurt people in the long run. Better he stay by himself—alone.

He poured the coffee and again thought of Mrs. Nelson and her cream. She seemed lonely, he thought. Like knows like, he supposed.

"It would do her little good to know me better, to share her cream and coffee. It's just better this way. Better for her. Better for Mary Beth." The words echoed back at him in the otherwise silent room.

"But what of you, Andy?" He could almost hear his mother's voice. *"Even the Lord said it wasn't good that man should be alone."*

He put the thought away, as if it were some unpaid notice of an overdue debt. "If the Lord thought it wasn't good for me to be alone, He should never have taken away the people I loved."

CHAPTER THREE

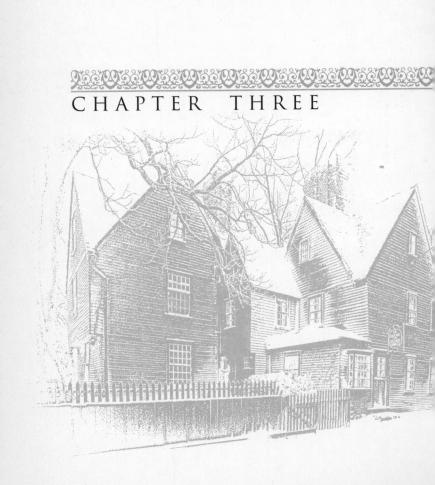

$\mathcal{N}$OVEMBER SPIRITS darkened with word that the 28th Infantry Division had recently been involved in a terrible battle. Information trickled in with no great reliability. Rumors ran rampant . . . and then the telegrams began to arrive.

Andy had never seen the likes. As Thanksgiving neared, there were more and more confirmations of the dead, and the community seemed to lose all hope as spirits fell to grief and sorrow. There was little to be thankful for.

All across town the tale was told in the stars. Blue changed to gold as heart after heart was broken in loss. Then snow fell with a vengeance, burying the town in white. But it seemed ill fitting. Its purity and freshness mocked the dark ugliness of war.

Then the news went from bad to worse. Most all of the 28th was feared dead or wounded on the fields of glory. The boys who once were going to stomp the Germans all the way back to Berlin now lay lifeless on the battlefields of Europe. The wind went out of the patriotic sails of Haven, Pennsylvania. The people had given their sons—their best— and the war had taken them and greedily demanded more.

In Bob Davis's barbershop, men gathered for discussions of war efforts and military strategies while the women met together behind closed doors for bouts of tears and prayer sessions. The town seemed to hold its breath in anticipation of what was to come.

Andy found himself working overtime to deliver all the messages. People seemed to watch out their windows for him. The white banners trimmed in red, bearing the stars of their loved ones, seemed like a beacon, pulling Andy magnetically to each house.

Blue to gold. Gold for death.

The cadence rang in Andy's ears as he marched through the snow. Once in a while there was good news. A telegram would announce that a soldier had been found wounded but alive and put in a military hospital. There was relief in such letters but also great frustration and anxiety. There was no possible way to go to their loved ones, to bridge the miles that separated them.

On the first of December, Andy went to work to find nearly a dozen telegrams already waiting. They were stacked neatly on the counter—innocent enough in appearance.

"They've been coming in steadily since I got here," the receptionist, Hazel, told Andy.

Eyeing the envelopes, Andy wanted to run in the opposite direction. Most of these telegrams were confirmation of the dead. There was no doubt about that. Two weeks ago the onslaught had been regarding the missing in action. The notifications now could only mean one thing.

Hazel worked on affixing message strips to plain paper. She seemed to have taken it all in stride. Andy wondered silently how she could sit there so peacefully, so perfectly at ease.

"Are any of them . . ." Andy couldn't finish the sentence.

Hazel looked up and shook her head.

"Most are confirmation. There are a couple of new missing in action."

Andy's spirits sank further. How much more could the little town take? Until a few weeks ago, no one had even heard of such a place as the Huertgen Forest, much less knew a battle there had stolen their loved ones away. People rushed for maps, for any piece of evidence to show where the fighting had been. The newspapers reported what they knew, but the details were so sparse it never answered the questions the people so desperately needed addressed. Did he suffer? Was it quick? Was he afraid?

The citizens of Haven craved information—demanded it—but there was often nothing to be had. The saying that "no news is good news" passed out of favor. Any news was better than being left to wonder in a state of near panic. Even the telegrams that would be delivered today would allow grieving families to know the truth about their sons, husbands, and fathers. It might be tragic, but it was better than never knowing.

Andy gathered the telegrams and headed out the door. The day was dreary; the clouds hung heavy and dark. The temperature dropped throughout the day as Andy made stop after stop. At noon he came back to find even more telegrams.

"Any sign of it slowing?" he asked the key operator. Hazel apparently was at lunch, as her desk was deserted.

The man shook his head. Andy couldn't be sure, but he thought there were tears in the older man's eyes as he added, "I think they got all of us."

The snow was now coming down in a blinding fury, a blizzard of massive proportion descending with a vengeance. The wind picked up, whistling through the trees, stinging Andy's face and eyes. He should just give up and go home, but he knew he couldn't. Folks deserved to know the truth as soon as possible.

The next telegram in his hand was marked to his high school principal. Andy hadn't gotten to know Mr. McGovern very well in school, but he knew the man from church, where Mr. McGovern was an elder and a member of the choir. He could still remember Mr. McGovern singing a moving rendition of "Silent Night" the previous Christmas.

Andy looked again at the message in his hand. He hadn't taken any telegrams to the McGoverns before, and he wasn't aware of any of the other delivery boys taking them either. Mr. McGovern's son Kyle was in the navy in the Pacific. He was a fighter pilot and everyone in the family was proud of his accomplishments. Several years Andy's senior, Kyle had been the all-American boy around Haven. He was the favored son in the McGovern household—a fine example of what a man could become if he put his mind to it.

Andy wearily climbed the snow-covered steps to the McGovern front porch. His hand trembled as he reached out to knock on the door. School had been cancelled for the day, so he hoped fervently that Mr. McGovern would be at home. He knocked loudly, solidly. It was a knock that announced importance— demanded attention.

The youngest member of the McGovern household, Amanda, came to the door. She was only ten, but she knew what Andy's presence represented.

"Daddy!" she cried and ran from the door in tears. "Daddy, come quick."

Mr. McGovern came to the door and opened the screen. He met Andy's gaze and stepped out onto the porch.

"Afternoon, Andrew." He seemed to age before Andy's very eyes. Shoulders slumped, the man reached out for the telegram.

For a moment time stood still. Andy felt he should say something—do something. He waited to see what Mr. McGovern would do and watched as his eyes filled with tears.

"He's just twenty-four," the older man whispered. "Just twenty-four."

Without warning, the big man, who had always seemed strong enough to bear the weight of the world, collapsed to the floor. Sobbing, he clutched the telegram against his chest. "He's just a boy . . . just *my* boy. Oh, God, help me."

Terror struck Andy's heart. He'd never in his life seen a grown man break down like this. He reached out his hand and then pulled it back quickly. How could he possibly comfort this man? Without waiting to see what else might happen, Andy turned and ran as fast as his legs could carry him.

Blinded by the snow, he pressed through

the storm, mindless of the remaining telegrams. When he reached the Jackson Street Bridge, he sought shelter under it. He gasped for breath while his heart pounded in his ears. Opening his mouth, he gave a primal scream from deep within his dying soul.

❧   ❧   ❧

Estella put her wartime cake into the oven and smiled. She hoped Andy would like it. She planned to take him several pieces tomorrow. Hopefully the snow would stop by then.

She looked at her watch and noted the time. It would take just under an hour for the cake to bake. That would give her plenty of time to finish her ironing and maybe even dust the front room.

Picking up the iron from the back of the stove, Estella tested it. She smiled as she noted it was perfect and hurried to the board, where her best Sunday blouse awaited her tender care. Many had been the afternoon she'd stood and ironed while her mother knitted sweaters for the war effort. Her mother had been good company after Howard's death—especially since Estella had no children. In fact, Estella wasn't sure she could have made it through without Mama's tenderness. Her mother understood what it was to lose the man she loved—she understood the loneliness and longing for companionship. Now Mama was gone and Estella was alone again. She tried not to be maudlin about it, however. God had a plan, even in this.

She smiled to herself. Yes, God had a plan, and she wasn't going to go getting weepy just because old memories were stirred up by ironing. Goodness, but she'd have to give up ironing altogether if she allowed such things to be a stumbling block in her spiritual walk. She laughed out loud. "I'd give up ironing—

wouldn't break my heart one bit."

Estella had just started to press the front of the blouse when a strange sense of urgency washed over her. Gone was the humor of the moment.

Andy.

It was the only word—the only thought— that came to mind.

Andy is in trouble. She stood silent, iron poised in midair, listening—waiting. *What is it, Lord? Is he in danger? Oh, please go to him. Comfort him, Father. He needs you so.*

A couple of days earlier, Estella had made a trip to the telegraph office. She'd inquired about Andy and obtained his address, telling the young man behind the counter that she planned to bake a cake and wanted to share it with Andy. She figured if Andy wouldn't come to her, she'd go to him. The only problem was, she didn't know where he lived. For almost two weeks she'd been trying to figure out exactly how to accomplish that feat and then it had dawned on her. Andy worked for the telegraph company. It should be fairly easy to find out where he lived. And it had been.

Now, however, she felt only the overwhelming need to pray for him. Putting the iron back on the stove, Estella hurried to the living room to retrieve her Bible. She sat down and opened the book to the thirteenth chapter of Hebrews.

"'Let brotherly love continue,'" Estella read aloud. "'Be not forgetful to entertain strangers: for thereby some have entertained angels unawares.'" She smiled to herself. Her husband had never known a stranger because of this passage. He'd brought home all manner of folk to share their dinner table and company.

"'Remember them that are in bonds, as bound with them; and them which suffer adversity, as being yourselves also in the body.'"

She looked upward. "Yes, Lord. Andy is in bonds—his heart is tied up tight and he suffers great adversity. You see him. You know where he is and how much he hurts. Lord, let me share his pain—let me help bear his burden. He's hardly old enough to carry it alone . . . like so many of our young men right now— boys, all of them.

"I can't help each one, but I can help this one." Estella's spirit calmed within her as she reread the same passage of Scripture.

"Oh, Andy. Please know that I care," she whispered, putting aside the Bible.

CHAPTER FOUR

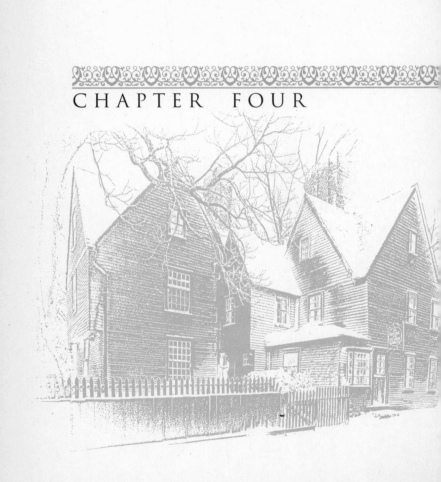

$\mathscr{A}$NDY COULDN'T remember how he'd made it back home. He could barely call to mind delivering the remaining telegrams after seeing Mr. McGovern break down. Now the entire thing seemed like a hazy bad dream.

Andy coughed and rolled over in bed. His foot pained him greatly. Not only that, but all of his joints ached and his head throbbed with a steady pounding rhythm. He coughed again, this time wracking his entire body. Struggling to sit up, his chest felt heavy.

I'm sick, he thought and fell back against his pillow. The reality of it began to sink in. *I'm sick and I'm not getting out of bed.* He pulled the cover high and moaned softly.

Maybe I'll die.

He thought of that prospect for several moments. Maybe he would die. Maybe he would die right there in that very bed. No one would even know about it for days, maybe weeks. He would be long gone before anyone missed him, and then it would only be the telegraph office that would question his absence. No one else would care.

He thought momentarily of Estella Nelson. *She would care—if she knew. She's that kind of lady,* Andy reasoned.

"But she doesn't know," he whispered and

gave in to another round of coughing.

He thought he should get up and at least telephone the office, but he'd have to go next door, and the prospect of getting up, much less getting dressed and actually going somewhere, was beyond comprehension. He chided himself for cutting off the telephone service to the house after his mother died. But there had seemed no reason to keep it. It was an added expense and the money was better spent elsewhere.

He tried again to sit up, but his chest hurt so much that he quickly abandoned the idea. *Let someone else play the Grim Reaper,* he told himself before allowing the sickness to draw him back into sleep.

⁂ ⁂ ⁂

Estella couldn't shake off the feeling that Andy was in trouble. The need to pray roused her repeatedly throughout the night. And pray she did. She prayed for Andy and for the other people in the town. She'd heard the news— read it in the paper. The town was in deep mourning.

When the clock chimed nine the next morning, Estella decided she could wait no longer. If Andy wasn't in trouble, then he'd be at work and about his business. But if something was wrong . . .

She packed up some of the cake and set it aside with her purse. Next she drew on her galoshes and coat, finishing up with a heavy scarf and gloves. She smiled at the winter wonderland that greeted her outside. The snow was at least a foot deep.

"It's just a little snow," she said aloud in the same manner Howard would speak upon rising to such a scene. "Snow will never slow me down." She mused over the memory of her husband shoveling snow in his shirtsleeves.

"Where's your coat, Howard Nelson?" she'd ask.

"Why? Is it lost?" he'd tease. *"Look, woman, I'm working out here. It may only be thirty degrees, but I'm sweating up a storm and I'm not wearing any coat."*

"Fine, then you'll just come down sick," she'd counter. But he never did. He had the constitution of a horse. Always able to get out there and do the job at hand. Until a heart attack changed all of that.

"Mornin', Miz Nelson!"

Estella smiled and waved. The little boys next door had come to shovel her walk and were even now finishing up the job.

"Good morning, Timmy. My, but we had a nice snow, didn't we?"

"Yup. School's closed for another day. Isn't it great?"

She smiled. "Just so long as you don't let your head gather cobwebs."

The boy looked at her strangely, but it was his little brother who questioned her.

"How would cobwebs get in your head, Miz Nelson?"

She chuckled. "Jimmy, any time you allow yourself to stop learning, cobwebs tend to gather. It's all well and fine to have a day off, but remember, you can always read a book and take a little adventure on your own."

"I don't like to read," Timmy interjected. "It's hard."

She patted the ten-year-old on the head. "It's hard because you don't practice. And you don't practice because it's hard. You have to try—you have to give it all you've got. I have to go run some errands right now, but if you like, you may both stop by my house later this afternoon. If you will come and read to me, I'll give you each a piece of cake."

"Real cake?" Jimmy questioned, his eyes widening.

Estella knew the family was very poor and completely unable to have such luxuries. "Real cake," she said, bending down. "And we'll send a piece home for your mom and dad. How about it?"

They nodded enthusiastically. "But what book should we read?" Timmy asked. "We don't have many books."

"That's all right. I have several that should interest you. Just come on over and we'll figure it out together." She paused and added, "And, boys, this is a first-rate shoveling job. I don't know when I've seen a cleaner sidewalk."

"Mama didn't want you to fall," Timmy offered. "She sent us over, but we would have come anyway. We didn't want you to fall either."

Estella laughed. "Well, we're all in agreement about that. I'll let you boys get back to work, but don't forget about this afternoon."

"We won't!" they declared.

The boys were quite excited and were still chattering about the prospect of cake as Estella made her way down the sidewalk. The folks in her neighborhood were poor, but loving and kind. They looked out for one another and they were especially good to her. Howard would be pleased to see it. He'd always worried about what would happen to her if he were to die first.

For a time, he had tried to teach her how to fix things around the house. She loved the memories of working with Howard as he fixed a smoky stove or mended a torn screen. She never gave any real consideration to learning to do the things he taught, however. Her Howard would no doubt be with her until the end of time—at least that was her plan. But not God's.

She smiled at the memory of Howard lovingly kissing her forehead and saying, *"Stella, you've been a good wife. I intend to see you cared for should anything happen to me. I can put money in the bank for you, but you'll save yourself a whole lot if you just learn to do the little things for yourself."*

He'd tried to invest wisely, but the Depression was hard on the country, and money slipped away as easily as ice melting on a hot Pennsylvania summer's day. There had been only a small savings remaining when a massive heart attack had taken her Howard away.

But Estella was a wise woman. At least she liked to think herself so. She quickly took what money she had and found ways to make it grow. First she rented out her house and went to live with her mother. She told herself it was for her mother's sake as much as for her own, but she knew the truth of it. Without someone around, someone to care for, Estella would grow old and bitter before her time.

Pittsburgh wasn't really to Estella's liking, but it was where her mother was happy. Her mother suggested Estella sell her house and stay permanently in Pittsburgh, but Estella knew she would never do that. No, someday she planned to go back to the home she'd shared with Howard. And so, with the economy continually growing worse, Estella took on sewing for a local tailor shop as well as nurturing vegetables in their backyard garden. Selling vegetables or trading them for other store goods, Estella and her mother didn't have to worry about food.

Little by little she added to the savings Howard had started. With their small house paid for, something Howard had insisted on doing back in the '20s, and a small pension left to her from Howard's job, Estella felt relatively safe and without fear of the future. God had always provided. Always.

Reaching the telegraph office, Estella went inside. She felt the dismal spirits of the employees, and her heart went out to them. A young man approached her with such a hang-dog expression that she couldn't help but reach out to him.

"Are you all right, son?"

He looked at her oddly for a moment, almost as if he found it impossible to believe she would ask such a question. "It's a hard day. It's been a hard week."

She nodded. "I heard that things weren't good. It must be especially difficult for you to be here and see all the sad news come in."

"Yes," he said, his voice barely a whisper.

Estella wanted very much to encourage him. "You have a difficult job to do—just as hard as the boys who've gone overseas. I'll be praying for you. Just know that you aren't in this alone. God is with you."

"That's what my mother says," he agreed.

"Well, she wouldn't lie—not to a boy so fine as you." Estella smiled. "Now, I won't keep you any longer, but the truth is, I'm looking for Andy Gilbert. Is he here or is he out delivering telegrams?"

"Andy didn't show up today. I couldn't tell you where he is," the young man replied. "He didn't call."

Estella frowned. "You don't suppose he's sick, do you?"

He shrugged. "Sick of the war, like all of us. The boss plans to stop by his house after work, but otherwise I don't know anything else."

Estella nodded. "Well, thank you for your time. Now, don't forget, I'll be praying for you and your friends here." She took her leave and headed back in the direction from which she'd come.

Oh, Lord, please let Andy be all right. He's all alone except for you—and now me. Help me to know what to do.

She prayed all the way to the street on which Andy lived. She had memorized his address and as quickly as her aging legs could manage through the deep snow, she made her way to his small house.

The blue skies overhead cheered her on. In spite of the cold, the sun shone down, warming her as she made her way. Snow capped each bough of the evergreens, sparkling and glinting in the sun. If she'd been fifty years younger she wouldn't have resisted the temptation to make a snow angel. She smiled as she imagined the comedy of a woman her age stopping to lie down in the snow to create just such a thing.

"No doubt they'd have me hauled off to the county home for the feebleminded," she mused.

With that thought still giving her cause to smile, Estella found herself in front of Andy's house.

"Seems like a nice place," she said as she observed the small one-story home. There was no sign that anyone had been about. Andy's walkway was deep with snow. "I'll have to be careful," she murmured. "Otherwise, I might end up making that snow angel after all."

She cautiously made her way up the walk, brushing the snow back and forth with her booted foot. It was a slow process, but it gave a hint of a clearing and helped Estella to better make her way. There were patches where ice had formed beneath the snow, making it even more risky, but her need to know if Andy was all right drove her forward in mock bravery.

Reaching the door, Estella knocked loudly. No one answered. She knocked again, but still there was no response. Reaching her gloved hand to the doorknob, Estella tried it. The knob turned and the door opened without any trouble.

She peeked her head in and called out, "Andy? Andy, are you here?"

She hated to just walk in but felt she had no choice. Something wasn't right. She was sure Andy would have gone to work if he were able.

"Andy?" she called again, now walking down the hall. She didn't even bother to take off her boots, figuring she would clean up the mess later.

Estella passed the front room and continued toward the back of the house. She noted the small kitchen and cold stove. The chill of the house was almost as bad as outside.

"Andy?"

She opened a door and found a bedroom. The coldness was worse here, as the room had been shut off from the rest of the house, shades pulled. As her eyes adjusted to the dim lighting, she could see that the room was neatly kept. The bed was made and the little dresser on the far wall had a neat arrangement of personal items a woman might use.

"This must be his mother's room," Estella whispered to herself.

Pulling the door closed, Estella crossed the hall to the only other door. This one stood ajar.

"Andy, are you in there?"

She pushed open the door and could see the outline of someone in the small iron bed. Coming across the room, she reached down to touch Andy's face. He was burning up with fever.

"Oh, Andy, I'm so sorry. I should have come sooner."

He opened his eyes but didn't really seem to see her. He moaned and coughed and then closed his eyes again, as if the entire matter had been too much effort.

Estella knew what she had to do. She quickly went to the kitchen. Pulling off her outdoor things, she mentally planned what to do first.

"We need some heat in this house," she declared. She looked to the stove and found a scuttle of coal sitting beside it. "Good. At least I won't have to go searching."

She quickly built a fire in the stove and put water on to boil. The steam would make it easier for Andy to breathe, and she could also use some of the water to make soup. "If I can find some ingredients," she said to herself.

She looked in the cupboards and drawers. There was such a small selection to be had and what she really needed was a fresh piece of chicken. Why, with that, she could make a nice pot of broth. Nothing made a person feel better faster than chicken soup.

After a futile search, Estella decided there was no other option but to go back out and walk to the store. She had her ration coupons and could probably get some small piece of meat. It wouldn't be much, as she couldn't afford much.

"Lord, you know what this boy needs. You know I hate to leave him here, but I must. Go before me, Lord," she prayed as she pulled on her coat.

The market was nearly eight blocks away, but Estella made the trip without any trouble. She prayed as she went and it seemed to make the time pass more quickly. To her sorrow, however, she found the store closed. The sign read: *Due to the death of our son, Tom, we will be closed today.*

She shook her head. "Poor folks."

"Mrs. Nelson? Is that you?"

Estella looked behind her to find the pastor leaning out the window of his car. He was a young man, generally full of energy and excitement. His smile had warmed her on many occasions, but today was not one of those days.

"Why, Pastor Bailey, what brings you to

town?" She walked to the vehicle as he stepped out.

"It's a sad time, as I'm sure you know. I've been making rounds and visiting with my flock. So many have lost children or husbands. It's truly a time of mourning for Haven."

Estella nodded. "I came to the market, but it's closed. They've lost their son, Tom."

"Yes, I know. I visited with them last night." He looked to the store window, then back to Estella. "What brings you out? It's very cold. Can I give you a lift?"

"I have a young friend who is desperately ill. I need to get a piece of chicken so that I can make him some broth. I suppose you could drop me off at the grocery store on Second."

"I can do better than that," he said. "I happen to have some chicken at my house. One of the farm families I visited yesterday gave it to me. I'd be happy to share my blessing with you."

Estella smiled. "I asked the Lord to go before me, and I see He has done just that."

"Indeed. He's always faithful, even in times like these." He helped Estella to the car and opened the door for her. "So who is your friend?"

"His name is Andy Gilbert."

He frowned. "I know Andy. He and his mother used to attend our church—at least until she became too sick. I visited her several times but then just seemed to lose touch until she passed on. Sad situation. I don't think there were more than a handful of people at the funeral." He went around and got in the car.

Estella shifted to look at him. "Why did you stop going to see them?"

"Andy seemed so hostile to my company. He even told me he wasn't interested in hearing about God. I think he blamed God for his mother's illness. He actually asked me to stop coming by, and I guess I found it easier to comply than to fight it."

"Still, it hardly seems right that everyone just let the boy go his own way. He has no friends—and it appears folks avoid him because of his telegram deliveries."

The young minister nodded. "Yes, I've heard that. Other delivery boys have mentioned such things."

"You should speak to the congregation about it," Estella said, feeling the need to point this out.

"I doubt they would hear anything I said on the matter." Bailey pulled into the parsonage drive and turned. "People are caught up in their own pain. I'm sure the delivery boys couldn't possibly have it as bad as the young wife or mother who has lost her husband or son." He opened the car door and quickly stepped out. "Now, you stay right here, and I'll bring the chicken to you."

Estella watched the slender young man make his way slipping and sliding through the snow. Apparently he'd had no time to shovel his walk before heading out on his calls.

She sat thinking about Pastor Bailey's words and knew that this was how most people probably felt. Of course losing a loved one couldn't be compared to anything else. There was no other cut that went quite so deep, or pain quite so sharp. Still, Andy's hurt was real—as no doubt was the misery of the other delivery boys.

The pastor reappeared, sliding his way back to the car. He'd almost made it back when his feet went out from under him and he disappeared from Estella's sight. She gasped and reached for the door handle just as he popped back up, red in the face but apparently no worse for the wear.

"I'm afraid this walk is more icy than I realized," he offered, climbing into the car. He handed Estella a small sack. "Here, I hope this will be enough."

Estella looked inside. "Oh my, but of course it will. I hope you kept some for yourself," she replied, noting that he'd given her two large pieces of raw chicken.

"I did. I'm not much for cooking, but Mrs. Parks from next door is always happy to help out."

Estella nodded. "Nadine is a good woman. I'm so glad to have made her acquaintance. Now, if you wouldn't mind taking me back to Andy's place, I'd surely be grateful."

"Of course," Pastor Bailey replied. "I consider this to definitely fall into my duties as a pastor. They give us extra gas rations, you know."

"The Lord always sees to His own," Estella murmured.

They rode in silence for several moments before Estella decided to brave revealing her thoughts. "You know, you have the ability to influence and encourage folks from your position in the pulpit. And as Christians, we ought to bear one another's burdens and give help to those in need."

"Absolutely!" he said with great enthusiasm. "I couldn't agree with you more."

"I know folks are hurting; just as you said, their own pain is so great they can't see the pain they're causing others."

"I'm sure you're probably right," he said with less excitement in his tone.

"I think you could go a long ways to help folks understand what they're doing. Especially with Christmas coming up and such. I hate to think that young Andy and others like him will feel ostracized throughout the holidays. Andy doesn't even have family members to gather him near."

They arrived at Andy's house just then and the pastor, appearing quite uncomfortable with the entire conversation, hurried around to assist Estella out of the car. "Let me help you. I see the walk here also needs to be cleared."

Estella refused to move. "Please hear me out. I may be an old woman, but I know what the Good Book says."

Pastor Bailey looked to the ground. "Mrs. Nelson, I know what it says too. I've tried to help this congregation, but as a fairly new pastor they often treat me like an outsider—even a child. I suppose because of my youth that's to be expected. Still . . ."

"Pshaw," she said, shaking her head. She got out of the car and stared the pastor dead in the eye. "You're called by the Lord. He expects you to walk boldly. I'm new to this congregation too. Howard and I used to attend church across town, where his mother and father brought him up. Still, I know what I know and I'm not afraid to tell folks that they're making a mistake in taking out their miseries on one another. These are hard times and we need to be working together, not tearing each other apart.

"The reports I read said the 28th Infantry Division has suffered great loss. That's going to devastate this town, as you already know. You're dealing with individual families right now. Encourage them to reach out to those who are hurting as much as they are. If they do this, their own pain will lessen. I know from experience that this is true."

"Well . . . it certainly makes sense."

"Of course it does. You can't spend too much time feeling sorry for yourself when you're caught up helping other folks with their problems."

They'd reached the door and Estella was anxious to get back to Andy. "Would you like to come in, maybe visit with Andy for a moment and pray for him?"

The pastor looked embarrassed. "I'm ashamed to admit I didn't think of it myself. Still, I wouldn't want to upset him."

"Andy's barely even conscious," Estella replied. "I don't think he'll mind that you've come to pray for him."

They entered the house, now considerably warmer than when Estella had left it. She noted that the water had almost completely boiled out from the cast iron kettle. "I'll need to add more water to this before we can see Andy."

"Here, let me help. I can get the water while you get out of your coat and overshoes."

Estella nodded and allowed him to take over the duties. She had just come back from hanging up her coat when Pastor Bailey completed filling the kettle. "Is there anything else I can do before we see Andy?"

"No, but when we're done, if you like, you could fetch me more coal. I would imagine there's a bin in the basement."

The young minister pushed back an errant lock of hair and nodded. "I'd be pleased to do just that."

They made their way to Andy's room. Estella was disturbed to see that the boy hadn't so much as changed position from when she'd left him.

"Andy," she called softly and put her hand to his forehead. "He's running a high fever. I'll have to work to get that down as soon as possible. Help me pull off this heavy quilt. He's just baking himself under all these covers."

Andy opened his eyes but said nothing. He didn't seem to even see Estella or the pastor.

"Poor boy was delivering telegrams in the snow yesterday. In fact, he's been out in the weather every day and probably has not bothered even once to take precautions to keep from getting sick."

"I'm sure you're right. When you're young,

you scarcely think of sickness and death." He paused and shook his head. "Well, at least that was true before the war. Now I'd imagine most every young person thinks of it. Why don't we pray."

Estella reached for the man's hand and then for Andy's. "I think that would be just the thing."

❧ ❧ ❧

That afternoon, Estella made the decision to return to her house and gather a few things in order to spend the night at Andy's. His breathing was still labored, and she was concerned that he would need to see a doctor if the fever didn't pass soon.

Leaving Andy in a deep sleep, she trudged the several blocks to her home with her heart quite heavy. *Oh, Lord, give Andy the will to live. Help him to see his importance in this world. Let him know that at least one person here loves and cares for him.*

She prayed for Pastor Bailey too. She knew the man needed God's strength in order to take on the burden thrust upon the shoulders of this community. "It can't be easy to preach encouragement and hope when things seem so far from good."

"Mrs. Nelson!" Timmy called, waving from his front porch stoop. "Can we come over now?"

Estella groaned. She'd totally forgotten about the boys. "Timmy, I tell you what, let me come over there. I have something to take care of and I can't stay long."

She saw the boy's crestfallen expression. "I'll bring you both an extra piece of cake to make up for it."

He perked up at this. "Okay. I'll tell my mama you're coming over."

Estella hurried into her house and took up

a small suitcase. Throwing in her nightclothes and personal items, she continued to pray.

"Lord, I want your will in all of this, but if it matters, my will is that Andy recover and learn to be happy again. You and I often see things the same way, so I'm praying that this is one of those times."

With her packing complete, Estella took up the remaining cake, grabbed a copy of *A Christmas Carol*, and headed next door. Timmy was waiting for her.

"Ma says you're to 'scuse the mess."

Estella laughed. "Your mama doesn't need to worry about such things." Just then the boy's mother appeared.

"Oh, Mrs. Nelson, Timmy said you were bringing cake over. You sure didn't need to do that."

"Now, now, Lois, I made the cake and surely can't eat the entire thing. I want you all to have it. I've saved a couple of pieces for another friend." She handed the dish over. "I also wanted to let you know that I'll be gone tonight—maybe a couple of nights. I'm going to tend a sick friend." She looked down at Timmy and Jimmy. "Boys, I'm so sorry to change our plans, but a friend of mine has come down sick. I need to go take care of him, but I've brought you a copy of one of my favorite books." She handed the volume to Timmy. "Maybe your mother would help you with the reading. The story is quite good and it's about Christmas."

"I'll be happy to read it to the boys," Lois said, then glanced past Estella. "How far do you have to go?"

"Over to Chester Street."

"That's a long way and the sun is about to set. Are you sure you want to walk all that way? My Charlie will be home from work at five and he could drive you over."

"No, my friend is all alone. I'm afraid he

might grow worse if I leave him too long."

"I understand. Now, don't you worry about a thing. The boys and I will keep a good eye on your place."

"Thank you, Lois. I knew I could count on you." Estella started to leave, then remembered the book. "Timmy, when my friend gets well and I get back, I'll sit down with you boys and we'll talk about the book. I'll tell you all about my favorite parts and you and Jimmy can tell me about yours. And maybe I'll make us some Christmas cookies."

"Oh boy!" Timmy exclaimed. "That would be a whole bunch of fun. I love cookies."

Estella laughed and leaned down. "Just between you and me . . . so do I." She winked and straightened. "Thank you again, Lois. The Good Lord knew what He was doing when He brought your family to this neighborhood."

The woman blushed. "Well, we don't have a lot of money, but we know how to be charitable with our time and efforts."

"And I believe that's far more important than just about anything else you could offer."

Leaving Lois and the boys, Estella hurried home to retrieve her things. Before heading out she remembered the sparseness of Andy's cupboards and grabbed a few of her own supplies to use for dinner and breakfast. *No sense taking undue advantage of the boy*, she mused. *Besides, I'm not at all fond of pork and beans.*

Andy was still sleeping when she returned. The house was dark because Estella hadn't thought to put on a light. She was grateful when the electricity came on without pause. Some folks in town had lost power, and she'd not even bothered to check earlier to see if Andy was one of them.

Slipping down the hall to check on Andy, Estella wondered at the life he led. People avoided him, and his whole family was gone. *He must be very lonely, indeed*, she thought. *I know exactly how that feels, Lord.*

She gently touched Andy's forehead and sighed. He was still hot. Burning from the fever and showing no sign of recovery. She'd once heard a doctor say that a person had to want to get well. Had Andy given up *wanting* to get well?

Estella whispered a prayer and went to work preparing soup and tidying the kitchen. Spying the spice rack, she was delighted to find a jar of dried garlic. It would add a wonderful flavor to her creation. She hummed a Christmas song as she worked, feeling so very useful and happy. This was as God intended it, she thought. No one should ever live off by himself. It wasn't healthy.

In the evening, Andy's boss from the telegraph office stopped by. Estella explained the situation and was relieved to find the man so understanding. After he'd gone, Estella settled down to do some mending for Andy.

Earlier in the day she'd washed some clothes for him and in doing so, she found that many items were in desperate need of repair.

I like doing this, she thought as she worked to darn a hole in one of Andy's socks. *I like to be useful—to be needed.* She sewed until it was nearly nine o'clock. Putting her things aside, Estella stifled a yawn. She wondered if Andy would mind her being here—spending the night. She'd already decided to sleep on the couch instead of the spare bed. Andy might not like the idea of someone else sleeping in his mother's room.

She quietly crept into his room and felt his forehead. He seemed a little cooler. Squeezing out a washcloth, Estella wiped his face and arms. Andy moaned and opened his eyes.

"Mrs. Nelson?"

"Yes, it's me. You just rest, deary. You've a high fever and I'm going to take care of you."

Andy closed his eyes. "I knew you would care."

Estella had no idea what he meant by the words, but since he'd already fallen back asleep, she had no chance to ask him about it. Perhaps he was dreaming about something else and Estella just happened into the picture when she began wiping him down.

She smiled at him, his red hair sticking out this way and that. He seemed so peaceful, and yet she knew he bore much turmoil deep within. *Lord, he needs to learn to trust you. To know that you are there for him, that you care, even when the rest of the world walks away.*

She bent down and kissed his forehead as she would have if he'd been her son. "Sleep well, Andy." She turned to leave but paused at the door. He seemed so lost—so frail. "Please get well, Andy. I need you. I can't begin to explain why, but I do."

❧ ❧ ❧

Three days later, Estella praised God when she found Andy sitting up in bed and feeling much better. His color had returned, giving a healthy glow to his freckled face.

"Are you hungry?" she asked as she came into the room with toasted bread, two fried eggs, and a cup of coffee.

"I feel like I could eat a dozen eggs," Andy declared as she put the tray in front of him.

"Well, two will have to do. There is a war on, don'tcha know," she said in mock disgust.

Andy actually smiled at this. It warmed Estella to see him looking so good. He dug into the food with great gusto. Estella sat down on the edge of the bed and smoothed the covers.

"I'm so happy to see that you're feeling better. I thought I might lose you that first night. Your boss stopped by to find out why you hadn't come to work, and I told him I wasn't sure you'd even make it through the night."

"I don't suppose I would have if you hadn't taken such good care of me," Andy answered between bites. He hesitated, seeming to struggle with the words. Andy finally whispered, "Although, I have to be honest, I didn't much care for sticking around."

Estella nodded. "I felt that. I don't think I've ever prayed so hard for anyone in my life as I've prayed for you."

Andy looked at her for a moment, then put down his fork. "Why? Why did you pray for me like that? Why did you come here and take care of me?"

Estella wondered how she could possibly explain. "I felt so strongly that you needed me." She choked back her emotion. "And, Andy, I need to be needed."

Before either one could say anything more, a knock came at the door. Estella pointed at the tray. "Eat and I'll see who it is."

She dabbed at the dampness in her eyes. *Lord, he can't possibly understand how much I want for him to heal—in his heart as well as his body. He can't possibly know how much this has helped to revive my spirits too.*

Estella opened the door to find Mary Beth Iseman. She knew the girl from church and was delighted to see such a welcoming smile. "Why, hello. Come in out of the cold," Estella told the girl.

"Mrs. Nelson! What are you doing here at Andy's house?" The young woman pulled off her scarf to reveal straight blond hair neatly pulled back and tied with a red ribbon.

"We got acquainted in the cemetery a couple weeks ago. How do you know Andy Gilbert?" Estella asked, reaching out to take the girl's coat.

"We went to school together, only he had to quit when he was a freshman. I was a year behind, but I always thought he was such a sweet guy."

"Andy is a sweet guy." Estella couldn't have agreed more. He was a sweet, gentle soul who deserved to love and be loved. She hung the coat up and returned to where Mary Beth stood warming her hands by the stove.

"So is Andy here?"

"He is. He's been very sick—influenza, I believe. He's much better now, however. Would you like to visit with him?"

Mary Beth nodded. "I feel like I need to talk to him. My mother . . . well . . . she wasn't very nice to him the other day, and I feel like I should apologize for her." She lowered her head. "I know a lot of folks aren't very nice to Andy. I know why too."

"Mary Beth, you're such a sweet girl. I know it would do Andy a world of good to have you visit. You just come along with me."

Estella led the way. Knocking on his

bedroom door, she called out, "Are you ready for a visitor?" She knew he'd be stunned to hear who the visitor was, so she quickly added, "Mary Beth Iseman has come to see you."

At first Andy said nothing, so Estella pushed open the door a tiny bit. "Andy?"

"Mary Beth is here?" he asked, the color once again drained from his face.

"She sure is. Do you want to see her?"

Andy looked down at the tray and then back to Estella. "I . . . uh . . . sure."

Estella beamed him a smile, then turned to Mary Beth. "He's just finishing breakfast. Come in."

Estella watched Andy as Mary Beth went to his bedside. "I'm so sorry you were sick. Mrs. Nelson said you're feeling better now."

Andy nodded and looked away. His voice cracked a bit as he answered, "Y-yes. I'm better."

Estella thought the young woman was

remarkably pretty in her blue print dress. A black belt cinched her waist, accenting her petite figure. "Andy should be up and around in another couple of days."

"I need to be back to work tomorrow," he said softly. There was no enthusiasm in his voice, however.

"Nonsense. You aren't recovered enough to go back to walking in this cold. They can spare you another day or two. I told your boss you'd be back when I decided you were well enough and not a moment sooner."

Mary Beth pulled up the bedside chair and sat down. "I think Mrs. Nelson is right, Andy. You need to get your strength back. I didn't even know you were sick, but now that I do, I'll do whatever I can to help."

Andy blushed. "Thanks."

They were silent for several seconds, and then Mary Beth launched into her speech. "Andy, I came here because I wanted to apologize for the way my mother acted the other day. I didn't realize until later that people were being so mean to you. My friend Anne told me that most folks avoid you because they're afraid you might have a telegram for them. They treat all the delivery boys that way. Mama explained on the way home that with Sammy at war, we were just asking for trouble to have you over. I told her I thought it was superstitious nonsense." She paused and grinned. "Well, I didn't exactly say it that way, but that's what I meant."

"It is nonsense," Estella encouraged. "God doesn't work that way."

"Exactly. That's what I said. I told Mama that God knew exactly which person would live and which would die and that it wasn't Andy's job to determine that. She agreed but said being near Andy only served to remind her that Sammy could be next."

"What complete hogwash," Estella said.

She saw the surprised expressions on the two young kids but stood her ground. "Well, it is. For people to alienate Andy solely because of fear or reminders of the war . . . well, they might as well get rid of their radios and stop eating. After all, ration coupons will remind them of the war as well."

Mary Beth giggled. "They'd have to tear down their black-out curtains too."

Estella nodded. "And sew cuffs back on their sleeves and pants. Oh, and we could stop saving fat and keep all our pots and pans to ourselves."

"Exactly!"

The two women burst into a fit of laughter. Only Andy remained sober. Estella came around his bed and gently patted his head as she would a small child. "I find Andy a pleasant companion—not at all a reminder of the war."

It was Mary Beth's turn to blush. "I do too."

Andy finally spoke. "Well, the entire town would call you crazy. I don't blame them for feeling the way they do—I blame them for the way they handle themselves, the way they act."

Estella nodded. "It isn't right. They are blinded by the problems and trials of their own lives. They cannot see or feel anything else. It isn't at all how God would have it be. God calls us to bear one another's burdens, to help those in need, minister to those who are suffering. People seem to have forgotten all about that."

"Well, maybe we need to remind them," Mary Beth said sternly.

Estella met the young woman's eyes. "Yes. Maybe we do."

CHAPTER FIVE

$\mathcal{B}$AKING WITH you is so much fun, Mrs. Nelson," Mary Beth told the older woman as they worked to make some Christmas treats. "My mother isn't interested in even putting up a tree this year. She's so worried about Sammy."

Estella pulled a pan of simmering raisins

and dates from the stove and poured them into a bowl. "I'm sure she is worried. It can't be easy to have him so far away, especially at Christmas."

"Bing Crosby was singing 'I'll Be Home for Christmas' on the radio, and I thought Mama was going to cry her eyes out. She finally stopped just before Poppy got home, but he knew just the same."

"I'm sorry to hear that. It can't be easy on you either. Sammy's your only brother, right?"

Mary Beth continued kneading her dough. "Yup, he's the only boy. He used to say having three sisters was a real pain in the neck." She sobered and met Estella's gaze. "But he didn't really mean it."

"Of course not."

Mary Beth's expression grew distant. "I'm scared something will happen to him. I'm afraid he'll get hurt . . . even die. I can't talk to Mama about it because she's just as scared."

"Something very well could happen, Mary Beth. It's the way things go with war. You have to accept the fact that Sammy is in a very dangerous place and he might get hurt—might not come back."

"I was hoping the war would be over by Christmas, like they talked about on the radio."

"Wishful thinking," Estella murmured. "I think that's everyone's favorite thing to say. Why, they were saying it after Pearl Harbor was bombed. With great patriotic indignation the boys marched off to war shouting, 'Remember Pearl Harbor!' while their folks sat at home and said, 'Surely it will be over by Christmas.' Everyone needs to have hope, Mary Beth. You too. It might not be over by Christmas, but it *will* eventually be over and done with, and we'll have our boys back home."

"Some of them won't be back."

Estella put her arm around Mary Beth. "No. Some of them won't be back."

"So many of the boys from Haven and the surrounding area are dead. It won't ever be the same, will it?"

"I suppose it won't," Estella replied. "But we must trust God. Even in this, He has a plan. Sometimes it's hard to remember that. Sometimes it's hard to have hope. But, Mary Beth, we have to have hope—hope keeps us going."

The young woman looked to Estella. "I'll keep having hope—if you will."

Estella smiled. "It's a deal." She looked at the table and gave Mary Beth one final squeeze. "We'd better get to work or all of this will go to waste. Then we'll have the government at our doors."

"That's right." Mary Beth giggled and crossed her arms against her chest in a purposeful manner. "Waste is out! We're at war!"

ᐊᑫᐧ ᐊᑫᐧ ᐊᑫᐧ

Andy went back to work the week before Christmas. There weren't as many telegrams now, but they came steadily nevertheless. As the week progressed, news came of a major German offensive in the Ardennes.

"What's that mean?" Bob Davis asked as he gave Mr. Harrison his trim. "What's an Ardennes?"

"It's a place, Bob," Ralph Moore threw out, getting up to go to the wall map.

Andy sat quietly waiting his turn in the barber chair. He didn't want to hear about another battle or another place where soldiers from the 28th might be fighting and dying.

"I don't see Ardennes on the map," Ralph announced, obviously feeling somewhat important, "but from what I've heard it's in Belgium."

"Reconnaissance in force," said Grandpa

Hurley suddenly. The man was of few words, but when he spoke, people listened.

"What's that, Gramps?" Bob asked.

"The Germans." He paused and looked at them as if those two words said it all. "Like old J. E. B. Stuart did at Gettysburg. It's a ruse to throw us off and test our lines."

They all nodded knowingly.

Andy looked up at the wall map. Bob Davis had put it up in January of '42, and it had proved to be a point of interest for anyone who wanted to know where the battles were taking place. They even used pins to mark where battles were or where their boys were stationed. Names like Corregidor, Midway, Guadalcanal, and Normandy were places now known in every household. Bob had always said it was a terrible way to learn geography. Andy agreed.

"Say, Andy, maybe you know where it's at," Bob suggested.

All gazes turned to Andy and the room went silent. Only the steady *tick-tock* of the clock could be heard. Andy didn't know what to do or say.

"I . . . umm . . ."

"Well, do you know where it's at or not? Don't they tell you nothin' over at the telegraph office?" Ralph questioned.

"Simmer down, Ralph," Bob said as he turned his attention back to Mr. Harrison. "I'm sure they don't just hand out that kind of information. You have to worry about spies and such. No sir, you can't just be telling everybody that kind of thing."

"Say, isn't it that place where the Nazis went through when they invaded France in 1940?" Mr. Harrison finally piped up.

"It's not an invasion," Grandpa Hurley threw out, stomping his cane emphatically. "Reconnaissance in force."

Bob completely ignored the old man. "So

is that where it's at, Andy?"

Andy felt his face grow hot as they all looked again to him for answers.

Ralph shook his head. "Seems like he oughta know since he's delivering telegrams."

Andy couldn't take any more. He got up and left the shop, barely remembering to grab his coat and hat. His haircut could wait for another day.

But the war wouldn't wait for anyone. The next day Andy found himself at work once again, trudging through new snow, taking the word to the townspeople. He dreaded his next delivery. Looking down at the letter in his hand, he grimaced.

Mr. William McGovern

This was the second telegram, and Andy had forgotten to ask if anyone remembered whether it was good news or bad. Dread settled over Andy. He climbed the steps to the McGoverns' and stopped in front of the wreath-decorated door. He took a deep breath and thought of Mrs. Nelson's words of encouragement.

"Your job is very important," she'd said. *"Whether the news is good or bad, not knowing is far worse. In the long run, folks will be glad to know."*

Andy knocked three times and stepped back. It was nearly five o'clock and he knew Mr. McGovern would be home. Seconds ticked by and still Andy waited. He looked at the missive in his hand and then to the banner that hung in the front window. The blue star seemed dull, almost washed out.

The door opened and Mr. McGovern met Andy's gaze through the screen. "Evening, Andrew." He pushed open the screen and reached out for the letter.

Andy handed it over, unable to move. "Evening."

The older man looked at the envelope. He

slowly tore it open and pulled out the telegram. Andy waited, watching and hoping. He didn't really understand why it was so important to know.

Mr. McGovern's eyes filled with tears. Andy's hopes faded and he turned to go.

"Wait, Andrew. It's good news. They've found Kyle and although wounded, he's alive."

Andy turned back. The star would remain blue—faded and washed out, but wonderfully blue. "I'm glad, Mr. McGovern. I'm so glad."

"Martha!" Mr. McGovern called out. "Martha, come quick!"

His wife, a short, stocky woman, appeared at his side. She bit her lip and turned her gaze to her husband.

"He's all right. He's in the hospital."

She broke into a sob, but these were tears of joy, and Andy felt almost blessed to have witnessed this tiny miracle. So often the doors were closed to him; he never saw the good along with the bad. How precious it was to be a part of the good. It bolstered him for what he knew was left to do that night.

"Andrew, come in and have some coffee with us. You must be freezing."

Andy stood momentarily stunned. No one had ever extended such an invitation. "Ah, no thank you, Mr. McGovern. I've got another telegram to deliver."

His former principal nodded. "I hope the news will be just as good as ours."

Andy knew it wouldn't be, but he said nothing. Nodding, he turned and walked down the steps. Twilight had settled on the town and soon it would be dark. There was only one telegram left. It was the one he'd been putting off.

Pulling it from his satchel, he looked down at the name.

Mrs. Kay Iseman

Word had come regarding Sammy. It was a

first telegram, so it would only announce that he was missing in action. It seemed a sick, demented game that the government played with people. Folks would wait in agony for that second telegram—the final word. Andy figured the military folk already knew who was dead and who wasn't, but by sending the first telegram they got folks ready for what was coming. The government might have thought it a rather merciful thing to do, but Andy just couldn't reconcile it as such. He'd seen the anxious faces, known that people were watching and waiting. During the time between telegrams, their entire world stopped. How was that more merciful?

Andy walked with deliberate slowness to Mary Beth's house. He could hardly stand to face her. She'd been so kind to him in the past, but now she'd no doubt feel the same as everyone else. She'd blame him for the bad news—maybe even believe her mother's superstitious ideas. Maybe he believed them him-self.

He made his way up to the large two-story house. Snow had been shoveled to the side, making deep drifts along the sidewalk. The lights shone from the front room window and reflected on the service banner in the window. Andy's stomach tightened.

He knocked on the door, wishing he could have been anywhere else in the world but there. *I'd rather be on the field of battle than here telling these good folks bad news. What will she think of me after this? How can she help but hate me like the others?* Andy felt a deep regret for something that might have been . . . but now would surely be put to death.

Mary Beth opened the door. Her face lit up with a smile. "Andy!" Then she looked down and saw the envelope in his hand. "Oh no." He saw the expression—the same one as all of the others. It was a mixture of fear, anxiety, and dread.

He looked at the envelope as well. "Is your sister-in-law home?"

"Kay! Mama!" she called out.

Andy looked up and saw there were tears streaming down Mary Beth's face. He heard her whisper her brother's name and it nearly broke his heart in two. He searched his soul for something to say—something to give comfort—but found nothing. How could he, the reason for her misery, also offer her consolation?

Kay was there first, with Mrs. Iseman close behind. They met Andy's gaze with a look of disbelief and then of terror. Kay shook her head as Andy extended the telegram.

"I'm sorry," he whispered.

Mary Beth's mother began screaming. "No! No! Not my boy!"

Mary Beth hurried to her mother's side—

never looking back at Andy—while Kay stoically gathered her wits, reached to take the telegram, and then closed the door.

Andy could still hear the cries and knew he was not wanted there. He was an outsider—their worst nightmare come true. Gone were the warm feelings from the McGovern house. The closed door said it all.

Andy walked to Mrs. Nelson's house. He was supposed to share supper with her tonight—he'd promised her. But he didn't feel like company. He didn't want to sit and make small talk about the day or about how the war was supposed to be over by Christmas. He especially didn't want to talk about Christmas.

He missed his mom and dad more than ever. This was his first Christmas without his mom and the loneliness of it was almost more than he could stand. Mrs. Nelson's faithful friendship helped soften the blow, but she couldn't be with him all the time. She had her own life and friends. She had church and other things that were more important.

He stood on the step and wondered if it might not be better to just go home. *But isn't this what you wanted? Someone to care, someone to welcome you inside so that you don't have to simply watch from the outside?* But even though it was true, Andy suddenly wanted to run away. He looked behind him to the street, then back to the house. Before he could change his mind, however, Mrs. Nelson peeked out the window and smiled. She opened the door and reached out to pull him in. Welcoming him as she always did with her gentleness and love.

"Andy. I thought you'd never get here. Come in and warm up by the stove."

Estella watched Andy as he shrugged out of his coat and hat. He had a look of complete defeat on his face. "What's wrong, Andy?"

"I had to take a telegram to Mary Beth's house."

Estella sighed. She could well imagine the sorrow in that house just now. "That was the first one you've delivered to them, isn't it?"

"Yes."

"So their boy is missing in action. We knew it might come to this. Remember what Mary Beth said the other day? She knew it was a strong possibility."

Andy held his hands out toward the stove. "But knowing that doesn't make it any easier."

Estella hung up his coat and set his hat on the hall table. *Lord*, she prayed, *let me speak wisely—speak for me.* She turned to Andy. "Come on. I have supper just about ready for us. I've made some stew. We can talk while we eat."

Andy said nothing and Estella knew he was deep in thought about Mary Beth. "I know you're worried about them," she said softly. "I'll go visit them tomorrow and let you know how they're doing."

His dark blue eyes closed as he stood there. "I wanted to say something to help, but I couldn't. I knew nothing would help."

"No, just then nothing would. Sometimes folks don't need to hear a word, though. Andy, you've got a big heart and eventually people are going to know this for themselves. I'm sure Mary Beth knows you care and that you wouldn't have wanted her hurt this way."

He opened his eyes and Estella could see they were wet with unshed tears. "No, I wouldn't have seen her hurt for the world. She's the only person, besides you, who's been nice to me since the war and all the tele-grams."

Estella knew the truth of it. "Let's eat our supper and you can tell me about your day." She motioned him to the chair opposite her own. "I'll pray first, if you don't mind."

Andy bowed his head without protest. Estella offered a brief but heartfelt thanks for their dinner. She asked too that God would go to each grieving family in their town and offer them solace. When she finished, she reached for Andy's bowl and began to ladle the stew.

"Do you really think God will comfort them?"

The question took her by surprise, but she tried her best not to show it. "Of course I do. Do you doubt it?"

"I just think if God cared so very much, He might not have allowed the war at all. He wouldn't take away the people we love if He cared about our comfort and wanted us happy."

Estella handed him his bowl. "I suppose that's one way of looking at it. It is a mystery as to why such things have to happen. I know my own heart nearly breaks when I think about all those young men dying for the cause of freedom."

"But don't you think God rather heartless to allow all of those deaths?"

Estella filled her own bowl, then looked up to meet Andy's questioning gaze. "The Lord giveth and the Lord taketh away. Who am I to question God?"

"What you really mean is who am *I* to question God. I know I haven't been living the way you do—going to church and all. I know that's the way my mama raised me to believe, but . . . well . . ."

"But it hurts to believe," Estella finished his unspoken thought.

Andy lowered his gaze and nodded. "It hurts."

"Oh, Andy, believe me, I know exactly what you mean. When Howard died I thought I'd never feel right again. My days were so lonely and my nights unbearable. I wandered through this house looking for some way to make things right, but nothing helped. We could never have children, so his presence didn't even live on in his sons and daughters. All I had were my memories."

"That's all I have—but they're not enough." Andy sank back against the chair. "Sometimes I can't even remember the good times. I think about how hard the years were prior to the war, how hard my father worked. I think about the hopes they had for me. My pa wanted me to do better than he did—to have more."

"He wanted good things for you. Every parent wants good things for their child."

Andy shrugged. "But he's gone and I don't know what those good things were. I don't know what it was he was working so hard to provide."

Estella smiled and thought of all she might have offered her own child. "He wanted to give you security . . . happiness . . . well-being. He wanted you to have a strong faith in the Lord, or so I would presume. Above all, he'd want you to love and to be loved. The Lord wants no less for you. After all, God is love."

"He doesn't seem very loving. Look at what He's done to His world."

"What He's done?" Estella questioned. "Seems to me that man's greed and lust for power started this war."

"But God is supposed to be all-powerful— all-knowing. Why not stop something like that before it got started? Why didn't He stop the car accident that took my father and left me lame? Why didn't he keep my mother from getting sick? Was it too hard for Him? Or did He just stop caring?"

Estella wanted to weep for the boy. She felt his misery—heard his anguished questions. *Oh, God, make him understand. Let him feel your love.*

"Andy, God loves you very much. He's never stopped caring for you. I know it's hard to believe that, but I have no doubts on this issue. The world may be at war, but it isn't happening because God doesn't care. God allows us certain choices, and those choices aren't always made wisely. Wars will come and go. People will live and die. It doesn't mean that God doesn't love us. This season of the year is a good reminder of that love. Christmas is all about God's love for mankind—for each person. And it's about hope. You mustn't lose hope, Andy."

"But I feel most alone *at* church. If God loves me so much, then why do I feel so rejected—so unloved? Especially there?"

She studied the redheaded boy for a moment. He looked so forlorn, so young. Here he was a man in full, but his needs were as great as those of a lost child trying to find his way home.

"Jesus felt rejected too. His best friends left Him when He needed them most," Estella finally said. "He knows how it feels to be an outsider, to have everyone shut their door to Him—to turn away. The night He was betrayed and turned over to those who would kill Him, Jesus experienced exactly what you're experiencing now."

She reached out and touched his arm. He met her gaze, his expression suggesting that he wanted very much to believe her. "Andy, Jesus knows the wound others have given you. He knows its depth and width. He knows the pain. But, Andy, He also knows how to mend this wound—how to make your heart whole again."

"I want to believe that," he murmured. "But I can't. If He felt this way—if He loves us—why would He ever allow us to feel like this?"

"Oh, Andy, He does love us. There's no *if* about it."

"I don't know what to do," he said, shaking his head. "I'm not good at figuring things out."

She smiled and put her hand atop his. "Start by being my friend—and let me be your friend in return."

He looked at her for a moment without speaking, then finally nodded. "I'll always be your friend, Mrs. Nelson."

"Thank you, Andy. I needed to hear that." And in truth, she did. For reasons that were beyond her understanding, she needed him. And without a doubt—he needed her.

CHAPTER SIX

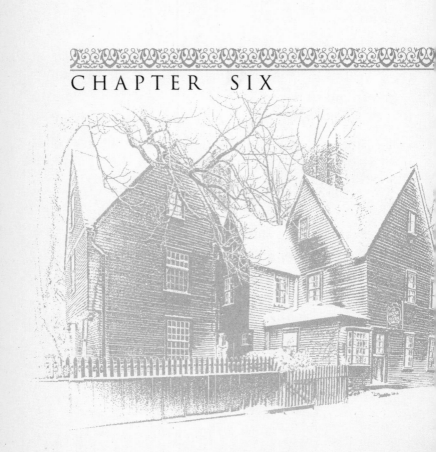

ESTELLA STOOD outside Andy's house and knocked on the door. She knew it was probably a futile attempt, but she intended to invite him to accompany her to the Christmas Eve services at the church that night. She'd already asked him once, but he'd wanted no part of it.

Mary Beth had encouraged her to try again. They'd seen each other at church earlier that day and Mary Beth had shared her sorrow over the telegram regarding Sammy. Estella offered consolation to both Mary Beth and Sammy's wife, Kay. Mary Beth's mother had taken to her bed and refused to even come to church.

"Mama's so afraid," the young woman told Estella when they had a moment alone. "I don't know how to help her through this because I'm just as afraid."

"You must pray for her and love her all the more," Estella told Mary Beth.

Now Estella felt the truth of her own words. She needed to pray even more for Andy—and love him.

Andy opened the door and noted the covered dish in her hands. "Come on in," he said, reaching out to help Estella inside.

"I wasn't sure if you would have anything

hot for supper, so I wanted to bring you a big bowl of chicken and dumplings. Just don't look too hard for the chicken. It's mostly dumplings."

Andy sounded weary as he answered, "If you made it, I know it's good." He took the dish and set it on the counter.

"It's a bribe," she said matter-of-factly. "I hoped I could talk you into changing your mind about church. It's going to be a nice service, I think. A special service for Christmas Eve. There's a memorial Christmas tree. The folks will hang gold stars on it for those who've been lost."

"Then they definitely don't want me there," Andy said, crossing his arms. "I've been the cause of most of those stars."

"No you haven't. That's been the job of the war."

"Even so, they'll remember me bringing

the news." He turned and walked away. "I'm not going."

"Mary Beth was hoping you'd be there. She's the reason I'm here now. She encouraged me to ask you again."

Andy paused and looked back over his shoulder. "Why would she do that?"

Estella smiled and shrugged. "I guess because she wanted you to be there. She's a sweet girl, Andy. I think she cares about you and doesn't want you to be alone tonight."

"Going to church isn't going to help that," he said, the bitterness heavy in his voice.

"Are you sure you won't change your mind? The service won't last that long, and afterward you could come to my house and have some cookies and coffee."

"I appreciate you asking, Mrs. Nelson. Really I do. But I'm not going. There's too much sadness already. Tonight those folks will remember their lost sons, and to see me still here and alive would break their hearts."

"But other young men will be there too. There are other boys who couldn't go to war. You aren't alone, Andy. Truly you aren't."

He looked up at her as if to contradict, then softly replied, "I'm not going."

Estella nodded. She knew it would be that way, but she'd hoped she might convince him otherwise. She'd even thought of playing on his sympathy, mentioning that it was a long cold walk to church and how she could use his company, but she refrained. "Well, I just wanted to try. I guess I'll head on over. I promised I'd help get things ready if I had time."

She moved toward the door, praying Andy would change his mind. *I just want him to see that he's really loved, Lord. I just want him to know that you are there for him, that you've never left him.*

"Thanks for the food," Andy said, coming

up behind her. "I wish you could stay and share it."

Estella put on a smile and turned to him. "Not tonight, but how about tomorrow—for Christmas? Why don't you come to my house and we'll share the day and maybe even find a game to play. I used to play a fair game of dominoes."

Andy looked at the floor. "It'd be nice not to be alone tomorrow."

She hated the dejection in his voice. No doubt he was thinking about his parents. This would be his first Christmas without his mom. Her first without her mom too. It wouldn't be easy for either one of them. Reining in her emotions, Estella replied, "Good. Then I'll see you in the morning."

Estella left feeling at least a small amount of satisfaction in having secured his agreement to come for Christmas. She didn't want to admit it, but the thought of facing Christmas alone was more than she cared to deal with. There had always been someone before . . . her parents, Howard. Last year she had strung pop-corn with her mother while they listened to Christmas carols on the radio. Despite the seemingly endless war there had been hope and joy and a certainty that God would soon bring the war to an end. They had prayed for just such a thing, and yet still the war raged.

She and her mother talked long into the night, sharing memories of days gone by. They spoke of the Great War, the war that was to end all wars. Sadly it had failed, and yet Estella's mother wasn't at all surprised.

"War will only end when Jesus puts an end to it," she said. Estella realized the truth of it and agreed.

Even now, the memories warmed Estella as she made her way in the cold night. She'd always had such a pleasant time fixing up the Christmas tree with her mother. This year, short of baking with Mary Beth, Estella really hadn't done anything to get into the spirit of Christmas.

I'm sorry, Lord. Here it is your birthday and I've not even prepared.

She thought of the service to come that night and wished fervently that Andy had come with her. The poor man felt he had to hide away like some abominable monster. It wasn't fair.

I know he feels rejected, Lord. I know he feels that the entire town of Haven has turned its back on him. I know in many ways they've killed his spirit. . . .

She looked up to the starry sky overhead. "That's it, isn't it?" Glancing at her watch, she made a decision. There was still time—if she hurried.

⚜   ⚜   ⚜

The little church had already started to fill up when Estella arrived. The organist played a soft medley of Christmas songs, and the music spilled out across the sanctuary as an embrace against the cold and hopelessness. Estella pulled off her scarf and glanced around, trying to decide where she would sit. Mary Beth quickly came to her side.

Hugging Estella, Mary Beth looked past her shoulder. "Is Andy coming?"

"No. He felt it would make everyone feel uncomfortable," Estella said sadly.

"I wish he were here. He wouldn't make me uncomfortable."

"I know," Estella answered, hugging the girl again.

"Can we sit together? Mama and Poppy are sitting over there with Kay and my sisters, but I'd like to sit with you too."

"It's good to see your mother here. Is she feeling better?"

"I don't know that she's feeling any more hope about Sammy's chances, but she felt it was her patriotic duty to be here."

"Why don't we sit just there," Estella pointed, "right in front of them."

Mary Beth nodded. "That would be perfect."

The service started shortly after the ladies took their seats. Pastor Bailey led the congregation in several songs. Estella's heart was moved when they began to sing one of Howard's favorite songs.

"'I heard the bells on Christmas day, their old familiar carols play,'" Estella sang, remembering Howard telling her that the song had been written during the darkest days of the Civil War.

"And in despair I bowed my head, 'There is no peace on earth,' I said, 'for hate is strong and mocks the song of peace on earth, good will to men.'"

Estella nodded knowingly. Those could have been Andy's words instead of Henry Longfellow's. The organ played a small interlude and then they joined in the final verse— a verse of hope. It was as if the author had come out of a black and empty place and into the hope that God offered.

"Then pealed the bells more loud and deep: 'God is not dead, nor doth he sleep.'" A tear trickled down Estella's cheek. No, God was not dead—He didn't sleep. He knew exactly what was happening in His world. He knew the pain of His children. He knew how they longed for peace—perfect peace.

They concluded singing and took their seats while Pastor Bailey faced the congregation. "Many of you feel the sorrow expressed in this song. You feel God must surely be asleep—that He doesn't care. Henry Longfellow wrote this poem during the Civil War. He needed to express the despair in his heart.

His son, a lieutenant in the war, had been seriously wounded in battle and only two years earlier he'd watched his wife burn to death while he tried in vain to save her life." He paused and looked from person to person across the congregation.

"He knew the sorrows of war and the pain of loss—just as you do. Tonight we've gathered to remember our losses—our sons and brothers, husbands and friends. Were it not for the war, they'd be sitting beside us at this very moment. Still, they are with us in memory." His words became more impassioned. "And I know in my heart they would be the first to tell you that God is not dead—He does not sleep. He's here with us now; He's never left us for even a moment."

Estella appreciated his words. It seemed God had given the young man a powerful understanding of the emotions and needs of the congregation. If only Andy had been there.

"We've put up a Christmas tree, and tonight we'll hang our gold stars on the branches to honor the dead. May it offer you comfort to know they are now out of harm's way, safely at home with the Lord. May it comfort you to know that God is with you always, that He walks this dark valley with you, never leaving you for even a moment.

"Christmas is a time to reflect on God's gift of love: Jesus. It's a time to remember that love and the love we have shared with those who've gone on before us. As we hang our stars tonight, I challenge you to remember that love rather than the pain and sorrow of loss."

The ceremony began with a representative from nearly every family in the congregation coming forward. As the stars were placed on the tree, Pastor Bailey read out the names.

Estella listened, hearing the names and the muffled cries in response. Mary Beth grasped her hand, and Estella could only imagine she was thinking of Sammy. *Oh, God, bring him back safely*, Estella prayed.

The organ played on softly and when the last person was headed back to his seat, Estella rose and walked to the tree. From her pocket, she pulled out a small gold star.

Pastor Bailey looked at her strangely. "I didn't know you had family in the service," he whispered.

She hung her star in plain view and turned to face the congregation as the pastor read out the name.

"Andrew Gilbert."

Whispered comments went rippling through the congregation. Finally someone from the back called out, "He's not dead—he's not even in the service."

"Well," she began hesitantly, "that is

where you're wrong." Her voice was soft and gentle, like a mother offering tender correction. She looked across the room, seeing each face—knowing they were all suffering, yet feeling confident that they needed to know what they'd done. "Andy serves, just as your sons and husbands do. He bears the weight of a war-related job, and because of what that job represents, you have shunned him, pushed him away as if he had caused your misery. In the saddest way you've taken his life as surely as war has taken the lives of the boys represented here."

Silence filled the room. Estella met Mary Beth's face and felt encouraged when the young woman nodded solemnly.

"He's just a boy . . . barely a man. Just like those we've sent across the seas. He needs love and companionship, but few of you have offered him much of anything but sorrow." She stepped closer to the front row.

"Is it his fault that his job should give him such a horrible task? Should he have suffered—been put to death in the spirit—all because your own pain is so great? Has any one of you stopped to realize that many of the boys who fought and died . . . were Andy's friends?"

She noticed Mr. McGovern. "Do you realize how Andy rejoiced when word came that your boy was found? Mr. and Mrs. Iseman, do you know how broken up Andy was when he had to bring that telegram about Sammy? It just devastated him." She looked back across the room. "He's just a nice boy doing his duty in the only way he can." Estella could no longer keep the tears from streaming down her face.

Mary Beth got up from her seat and came forward. Standing with Estella, she put her arm around the older woman in support.

"She's right, you know. Andy is one of the sweetest people I've ever known. He had to quit school when he was fifteen to go to work after his father died. I'm confident he never complained about it because that's not the kind of person he is," Mary Beth said softly. "But I do know he's in pain all the time. I've seen him grimace when he walks. His own injury from the accident and then losing his folks have left him hurting."

For several moments no one said anything. Estella looked at the congregation, desperately hoping she had gotten through in some small way. They stared at her in stoic silence. Even Pastor Bailey didn't know what to say.

"There's a young man who is sitting alone tonight—on Christmas Eve," Estella told them. "He has no one to comfort him, no one to share his fears. You'll all go back to your homes and share your pain together. You'll hope and pray and dream of better times while that boy is swallowed up in the sadness that has become his life. I don't think it would be possible for me to stand before my Lord—to look Him in the eye—if I did less than extend the hand of friendship to one of His own."

Estella headed toward the door with Mary Beth on her arm. They paused momentarily at the pew where the girl's folks sat.

"Mama, Poppy, may I go with Mrs. Nelson?"

Her mother sat with her head bowed, but her father looked up and nodded. "I think that would be fine."

Estella was proud of the girl. She had no idea what the future might hold in store for Mary Beth and Andy, but she thought they'd make a fine couple. Maybe the Lord thought so too. She smiled to herself and began to hum. It was a beginning.

CHAPTER SEVEN

ANDY OPENED the door to his mother and father's bedroom. The cold air rushed out, leaving him chilled. He switched on the light and looked around for a moment. The linoleum floor bore several rag rugs and at the window hung curtains his mother had made only a few years before the accident. Across the room his parents' bed stood. It seemed small—cold.

His mother's good friend Harriet had stripped the sheets and remade the bed with fresh linens after they'd taken Andy's mother away to the funeral home. She said he'd feel better knowing everything was in order. He didn't.

After that day, he'd closed the door and had never gone back. Today was the first time. He hesitated. It almost seemed to be sacred ground. Here his parents had shared their most private moments. Here they had talked about their hopes and dreams.

His father had papered the walls in a flowery print after his mother had spied it at the store one day. Confiding in Andy, his father had said he actually hated the pattern and would have preferred to paint, but that Andy's mother had so loved it that he couldn't help but love it too.

That was the kind of love they shared.

They were truly one. One in spirit, one in flesh, one in heart.

Andy had never known more love and security than he had experienced here in this room. He warmed a bit at the memory. In this room he had been a little boy—a much-loved son. He had held no responsibilities and no worries. His father had provided for them, and his mother had seen to his needs. He'd been safe and well loved.

He caught sight of the reason he'd come. His parents' Bible sat on the stand beside the bed. He crossed the room, feeling silly for the sensations that washed over him. He glanced over his shoulder nervously, almost as if a ghostly image of his mother might appear before his eyes.

He took up the Bible and hugged it to his chest. He couldn't explain his action, but it made him feel better.

He walked to the door and looked back

again to the room. Happy memories came to mind—memories of coming here on Sunday mornings when he'd been a little boy. He'd been allowed to crawl into bed with his mother and father on cold winter mornings. Together the three of them would cuddle and talk about the day and then get up and ready themselves for church.

He could almost hear his childish squeals of laughter as his father tickled his ribs to motivate him out of the warm bed. Andy smiled broadly at the thought.

"Time to go, Andy my lad," his father would declare.

Andy jumped. His father's words hung on the air—at least they seemed to.

"Oh, I wish you were both here—alive and well. I wish you could be with me tonight and help me through my fears."

The words echoed in the silence of the room. The empty bed seemed a lonely reminder that they were gone for good. They were not coming back.

Andy turned the light off and then shut the door once again. He looked at the closed door and sighed. "I wish I were eight years old again and I wish this stupid war had never come."

He reached out and fingered the handle. A part of him longed to go back into the room, curl up on the bed, and never again face the world. Why couldn't things be good? Why couldn't they be the way they once were?

"If only I'd died in the accident with you, Dad. Then we'd all be in heaven—we'd all be happy." Death seemed such a kindness at this point.

With shoulders slumped, Andy made his way back to the kitchen. He sat down at the table and placed the Bible in front of him. How many times had he seen his mother with this black book in her hands? Since his father's

death it had definitely been a daily event—
maybe more.

*She found such comfort here—such hope.
Mrs. Nelson feels that way too,* he reasoned. *I'm
sure for them it must have made a difference, but
I don't see how it can help me.*

He opened the book and flipped through
the pages. *There's nothing here that will make
sense of the war or the pain and suffering that's
going on. There's nothing here that can make it all
right.*

His gaze was fixed on the upper right-hand
corner of the page when Isaiah 53 came into
view.

*He is despised and rejected of men; a man of
sorrows, and acquainted with grief: and we hid as
it were our faces from him; he was despised, and
we esteemed him not. Surely he hath borne our
griefs, and carried our sorrows: yet we did esteem
him stricken, smitten of God, and afflicted.* Tears
began to stream down Andy's face.

He knew. Jesus knew.

He knew what it was to feel completely despised—rejected. He knew what it was to have people turn away, to hide their faces from him.

He knew the pain in Andy's heart—the deep wounds that others had given him. Wounds that he didn't ask for, precipitate, or deserve. Through the blur of his tears, Andy read on.

But he was wounded for our transgressions, he was bruised for our iniquities: the chastisement of our peace was upon him; and with his stripes we are healed. All we like sheep have gone astray; we have turned every one to his own way; and the Lord hath laid on him the iniquity of us all.

His tears fell onto the pages as he bowed his head and wept silently.

"I've gone astray. I'm just as guilty as those who wounded you, Lord." From deep within, the ice that encased his heart began to crack and fall away. "I'm worthless. I've despised you and rejected you. Oh, God, I'm so sorry."

The truth awoke in him an overwhelming, stabbing pain. It permeated his entire being. All the misery he'd tried so hard to shield himself from—the sorrow he'd tried to ignore—it was all there.

God, this hurts so much.

He saw the faces of his neighbors and former friends. He saw their fear. The blind raw fear that dictated their actions. His heart pounded, threatening to burst.

But it wasn't just this. "It's not just the people in town—it's not just the way they've acted toward me. It's the war . . . my friends are dead."

Another reality he'd not given validity to. This truth had been buried deep inside along with the images of those boys he'd grown up with.

Ray Masters, Jerry Gilpatrick, Brian Connors,

the Harrison boys . . . and so many others. *We'll never play baseball again at the Fourth of July celebration. We'll never go fishing off Crawson's Bridge.*

In his mind, Andy could see each of his boyhood friends—smiling, laughing, just as they were before they went away to war. *Why should they be dead while I'm still alive?*

Then came the guilt. Suppressed and black, hardened with age. "Oh, why am I still here? I could have died in the accident. I should have died." With the look of each mother who'd joined the gold-star club, Andy saw the accusation—the glaring question: "Why wasn't it you instead of him?"

Then suddenly Andy realized it wasn't their accusation at all. He was seeing a reflection in their eyes of the questions that he held in his own heart.

The purging went on as years of rotten

bitterness, putrid envy, and aloof disregard came surging upward.

But he was wounded for our transgressions, he was bruised for our iniquities: the chastisement of our peace was upon him; and with his stripes we are healed.

The words echoed in Andy's mind. *He was wounded for our transgressions. . . .* Jesus bore it all. The guilt, the insult, the misery and bitterness. Andy could almost visualize the scene—Jesus nailed there to the cross.

Andy raised his head and whispered, "And with his stripes . . . we are healed."

He struggled to regain his composure. Sitting up, wiping at his eyes, Andy wondered if such healing could really be had. He looked at the words again, trying hard to take them in, to understand.

Startled to hear voices outside his door, Andy got to his feet before anyone could knock. He opened the door, throwing it back in almost wild abandonment, to find Mrs. Nelson and Mary Beth. For a moment they exchanged a glance—almost as if each party knew that there had been an important break-through that evening.

Finally Mrs. Nelson was the one who spoke. "Andy? Are you all right?"

He motioned them to come in. "I've been reading."

"Ah, well, it's a good night for that," Estella said, heading into the kitchen.

"What were you reading, Andy?" Mary Beth asked.

Andy motioned them to the table. "Isa-iah."

The women exchanged a look. Andy knew they were surprised, so he hurried on to explain. He needed to tell them everything before it spilled over and reduced him to a blubbering ninny. "I've felt so long that there was no reason to go on. Life is just so hard, and the way folks made me feel—the way I made myself feel . . . I didn't think I could go on."

"But now?" Estella asked, meeting his gaze.

Andy looked deep into her eyes. "Now it's different. Those verses made it different."

Mary Beth stepped closer. "How, Andy?"

"He knows how it is," Andy whispered. "He knows what I'm feeling because they did it to Him too." His voice took on a tone of awe. It was all just really starting to sink in and make sense. "You tried to tell me, but I didn't understand. It didn't seem possible, but it's all there. They despised Him."

"Who?" Mary Beth's voice was barely audible.

The word came from Andy's mouth in complete reverence. "Jesus."

Estella went to the open Bible as Andy continued. "It says there He knew what it was to be despised and rejected. To have people turn away—even hide their faces from Him. He knows how I feel—what I've gone through."

Mrs. Nelson nodded. "Indeed He does."

Andy went to her and Mary Beth followed. "You tried to show me that—to tell me about Jesus and how His friends deserted Him. But I just couldn't see it until I read it there in chapter fifty-three."

Andy noted they were still wearing their coats and hurried to remedy the situation. "I'm sorry. Here I am just talking and talking and you're standing here. Let me take your coats and then you can sit down."

Mrs. Nelson smiled. "Andy, you never have to worry about such things." She handed over her coat and scarf. Mary Beth did likewise.

Andy hung the coats on a hook by the back door. "I need to tell you both that I prayed. For the first time in a long time, I really prayed." He turned back to find a look of satisfaction on Mrs. Nelson's face.

"And what did you pray for, Andy?" she asked.

Mary Beth took the seat beside her at the table and nodded. "Yes, what did you pray for?"

Andy joined them. "Forgiveness." He sat down opposite the women and closed the Bible. "I prayed for forgiveness."

Estella wanted to sing and shout all at the same time as she listened to Andy talk of how God had broken through the hardness of his heart. *This is all I wanted for him, Lord. Just to know your peace and love—to feel that there was hope.*

"I just got wrapped up in my own selfish need," Andy said softly. "There were things I wanted, I needed—and so many losses in my life. I felt like God was robbing me . . . like He was a thief in the night stealing away all the people and things I loved."

"Sometimes God needs us to put our house in order," Estella said. "He works to help us eliminate the clutter. Not by taking away loved ones, but rather by showing us ways to rely more on Him and less on the world."

"I remember my mother and father talking about that," Andy said, nodding. "I guess I really miss them most of all. I sit here alone and the house seems so empty, so sad. I really hate it. I never knew that until tonight. I had thought the house actually helped me feel closer to my folks, but instead it just reminds me that they're gone. I was in their room tonight, and while special memories came to mind, the pain was all fresh."

Andy's thoughts continued to pour out. "I remember the last Christmas we had together. Dad and I went together to buy Mom a special blue plate that she wanted. I'd saved up to buy it, but I didn't have quite enough. Dad paid the rest and we agreed it'd be from both of us. About a month after Mom died, I accidentally broke that plate. It was like losing her all over again."

Andy looked so forlorn Estella wanted to comfort him, but she held back. She felt it was important that he express all of these emotions.

"Having my mom and dad die," Andy finally continued, "is the worst thing that's ever happened to me. I'm still not sure how to deal with it—even now."

"When I was a little girl," Mary Beth said, "I remember thinking that the worst thing in the world was to be poor. We had more than some because we lived on a farm, but I would see the things my friends owned and wish I could have more than I had. Every Christmas my folks would do their best to make sure we had something under the tree, but it was never much and never what I really wanted." She paused and sighed.

"I know that sounds terribly selfish," she went on. "I don't like to admit it, but it's the truth. Now I'd just like to have Sammy back safe and sound. Now the worst thing is having him gone and not knowing if he'll ever come back."

"The worst thing to me was losing my dear husband." Andy and Mary Beth looked to Estella and nodded as though they understood. "I married quite young; I was only sixteen. Howard hung the moon and the stars as far as I was concerned. He was a handsome man," she remembered with a smile.

"He was also very prudent. Saved money and paid cash for everything. We never did without, and every Christmas was always quite special. Howard always liked to surprise me with special little gifts. He treated me like a queen." She paused and bowed her head.

"Then one day, he was gone. Just like that. No warning. No second chances. No last farewells. But you know," she met Andy's gaze, "for all the pain of losing him, I wouldn't trade for a minute what we had. The loss is hard, but it would have been harder still to have never had him in my life—to have never known his love."

She looked to Mary Beth. "We have no way of knowing what will happen in the future. Sammy may be found and come home. Or he might not return to you again. But having had him in your life for the years God has already given is a precious gift that you must never trade for sorrow."

"I won't. I promise," Mary Beth declared adamantly.

"And, Andy, I know your loss is great. My own dear mother passed away just months ago. I don't think a child ever gets over losing a mother. After all, mothers are the ones who give their children life—they're the ones who dry their children's tears and tuck them in. Losing a mother is like losing a part of yourself. And losing your father . . . well, that to a man is an overwhelming moment. It's a passing of the mantle of responsibility. It's facing mortality, and it's hard. Sons look to fathers as their pillars of strength and stability. When that's gone . . . well, it's difficult, to say the least.

"As I look around us at the community, I see a number of children who will grow up without their fathers. Most are younger than you were, Andy, when you lost your father. Some barely even knew their fathers. They will suffer this loss deeply, and we must always be mindful of that."

Andy agreed. "I wish this war would end. I'm so—"

Just then there was a commotion outside the house. A knock sounded at the front door, and Andy's expression registered surprise. "Who could that be? All my friends are here." He looked at Estella and Mary Beth, almost as if he wondered what he should do.

Estella shrugged. "You won't know unless you go see."

Andy nodded and reluctantly got to his feet. He looked almost scared. Estella got to her feet. "I'll come with you."

"Me too," Mary Beth declared.

They went to the front door together. Andy opened it and looked out. "It's like the entire town is here." He stepped back a pace, unsure if they might do him harm.

Estella looked out and felt her chest tighten in the emotion of the moment. "No, it's just the church. Your church, Andy."

He opened the screen door and was greeted by Mr. McGovern. "Andrew, we've come to say how sorry we are." The man's eyes filled with tears. "It wasn't until tonight—

until I heard Mrs. Nelson speak at church, that I realized how bad things were for you. How we'd caused you so much pain."

"I don't understand," Andy said, looking to Estella and then back to Mr. McGovern.

Estella reached for Andy's hand and gave it a squeeze. "It's Christmas Eve—a night for miracles."

"Andrew, we were mindless of the way we were treating you. When word came that our boys were wounded—dying—it was far easier to blame you for the bad news," Mr. Harrison said, moving forward. Mrs. Harrison was on his arm, nodding, crying.

"We were wrong," Bob Davis added.

"Yes," came the murmured voices of a dozen or more people.

Mr. McGovern reached out to grip Andy's shoulder. "We've come to ask your forgiveness, son."

Estella stood in the wonder of it all. A

night of forgiveness . . . a night of healing. She saw the gleam in Andy's eyes. It was a light of hope.

"I don't know what to say," Andy mumbled. He looked down at the ground, tears threatening to spill from his eyes.

"Forgive us, Andy. Forgive our blindness and our cruelty. Forgive our ignorance," Mr. McGovern replied. He pulled Andy into a bear hug and Estella dropped her hold on Andy's hand. Things would be different now. Andy would never again be alone—of that she was certain.

Smiling, she stepped back and looked at Mary Beth. The young woman seemed mesmerized by the unfolding events.

One by one the folks from the Eleventh Street Methodist Church came forward to hug Andy and give their apologies. When they'd all left except for Mr. and Mrs. Iseman, Mary Beth stepped forward. She'd gone and retrieved her coat and now was ready to say good-bye.

"I need to go home with my folks," she told him.

"First, I need to say something," her mother declared, stepping forward. "Andy, I'm sorry for the way I behaved in the store. It was wrong of me and I'm very much ashamed. I wondered . . . if you might join us for Christ-mas dinner tomorrow." She looked past him to Estella. "You too, Mrs. Nelson."

"Why, that sounds like great fun. What do you think, Andy?"

He looked to Mary Beth and smiled. "I'd like that . . . a lot."

"Good. I'll expect you both around two," Mrs. Iseman told them.

Mr. Iseman shook Andy's hand. "Glad you can make it."

As Mr. and Mrs. Iseman started down the walkway, Mary Beth reached out to give Andy a hug. Then she surprised both Estella and Andy by planting a kiss on Andy's cheek. "Someday," she whispered, "the war will be over and the sadness will be behind us. Someday there will be room for happiness and joy again." She started to go, then turned at the door with a smile, adding, "And maybe . . . love."

She left quickly after that, giving Andy no chance to speak. Estella watched the play of emotions on the young man's face. *Yes,* she thought, *maybe there will be room for love.*

CHAPTER EIGHT

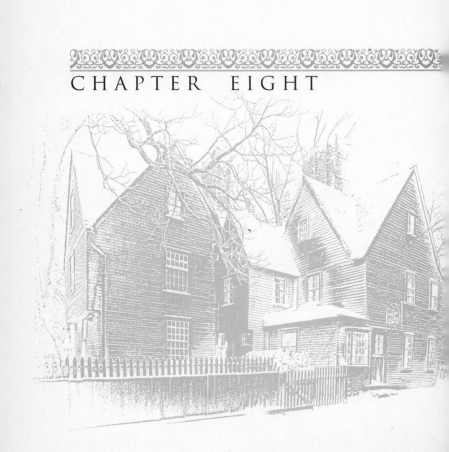

OR THE FIRST time since losing his mother, Andy allowed himself the privilege of feeling loved and blessed. He thought it was what she would have wanted for him, remembering that even as she grew more ill she had told him that her dearest wish was that he would be happy.

Slipping away to the cemetery before joining Mrs. Nelson for Christmas brunch, Andy felt the weight of his misery slip away. God had taken the burden from Andy's shoulders and now bore it in Andy's stead.

Pushing back the little wrought-iron gate, Andy walked into the snow-covered cemetery not with a heart of sadness, but with one of liberty—freedom.

He paused at his parents' headstones and bent down to brush away the new snow. He then dusted off the pine wreath and adjusted its placement between the markers.

"I know you're both in heaven—certainly not here in the ground." He then looked skyward, the brilliant crystal blue almost hurting his eyes.

"I miss you, but you'd both be pleased to know that I'm going to be all right. I couldn't say that a few weeks ago. I wasn't sure I would ever be anything more than the mess I'd made of myself. But now . . . now I have a new confidence in God. I will still miss you, still think about you every day. But I know where you are. And one day, I'll be there too."

❧ ❧ ❧

Later that day as they made their way to Mary Beth's house, Andy told Mrs. Nelson of his visit to the cemetery. "It wasn't like before. If you hadn't wandered along that other time, I think I would have lain down and died right there and then."

"God knew what we needed."

"We?" Andy looked up at her. "What do you mean?"

Mary Beth came out of the house to greet them. "Merry Christmas! Come inside and get warm!"

Estella squeezed Andy's arm. "I'll tell you later."

Andy smiled at the older woman. She was such a sweet, gentle soul, so very much like his mother.

The day passed in joyful celebration. Kay had gone to spend the day with her parents, leaving just the Isemans and their daughters. Mrs. Iseman was in particularly good spirits.

"My best friend, Melba, heard that her boy is safe," she told them as they sat down to the table. "I've decided not to borrow trouble regarding Sammy. I know that no matter what happens, it's all in God's keeping and I can trust Him for the outcome. I know too we'll all band together if the worst does happen."

Andy looked up to meet her gaze. There was peace in her expression, a peace that matched his own heart. Tomorrow he would again take up his job and deliver telegrams. Again he would be the bearer of bad tidings. But somehow things had changed. He knew it would be different—not because anyone else was different, but rather because he had changed.

They shared a wonderful meal in spite of the war rations and shortages. Mr. Iseman had managed to obtain a nice pork roast for their holiday feast. His brother, who had taken over the farm, had insisted on sharing part of their bounty. There were fried potatoes, creamed corn, and pickled beets. Mrs. Iseman had made fresh bread, and Estella had brought some wonderful cookies that she and Mary Beth had concocted one afternoon.

Andy ate until he knew he couldn't possibly eat another bite. Never had anything tasted so good. One by one they told stories of Christmases past, of Sammy, of better days. After the meal was cleared away, they gathered around the piano and Mrs. Iseman played Christmas carols while they all sang.

The afternoon slipped away from them and soon evening darkened the skies. Just as they were gathering their coats, Mary Beth came forward with a little knitted bundle.

"This is for you, Andy," she said rather shyly.

Andy took the gift and unfolded it. It was a hand-knit scarf. The light blue color matched Mary Beth's eyes. "It's wonderful. Did you make it?"

She nodded. "I knew your old one was pretty thin."

Andy wrapped it around his neck and nodded. "This is much warmer. Thank you."

Mary Beth smiled and looked down as if embarrassed. Andy knew it would take very little to lose his heart to her. Maybe there *would* be time for love . . . in spite of the war.

Helping Mrs. Nelson into her coat, Andy thanked the Isemans for their invitation. Then Mrs. Iseman hugged him. "Be safe, Andy. And don't be afraid when you come here next time with a telegram. No matter the news, I won't blame you."

Andy choked back his emotion and nodded. "Thank you."

Andy helped Mrs. Nelson down the stairs and continued to hold on to her arm as they made their way back to her house.

"It was a marvelous day," Estella said, looking up at the night sky. "You've given this old woman a precious gift, I hope you know."

Andy looked at her oddly. He'd given her nothing—in fact, he'd felt quite remiss for not at least wrapping up something of his mother's to offer her for Christmas.

"I don't know what you mean."

"I mean you gave of yourself, Andy. You gave your time and your heart. For years I begged God for a child, a son. It was like a thorn in my flesh that I could never have children." She paused as they reached her house. "I know you belong to others, but in a small way, I feel God has given you to me."

Andy felt a warmth spread over him. "I feel the same way. I wasn't ready to be without a mother. God knew that and sent you into my life."

Estella's eyes filled with tears. "I'd like very much to be there for you in whatever way you need me, Andy." She paused and seemed to struggle with what she wanted to say next. "Andy, I don't know how you might feel about this, but I'd like to make a proposition."

"Go ahead. You have my complete attention." She'd stirred his curiosity.

"I have this big old house all to myself— and there is a war on, don'tcha know." She smiled and gently squeezed his arm. "I'd like you to come here and share my home—if you're of a mind to do so. I'd like to cook and clean for you, to take care of you . . . until you convince that sweet Mary Beth that it's her job to do so."

"Mary Beth?" Andy asked uncomfortably.

"Why, she's just a friend." He didn't sound convincing even to himself.

Estella looked up at him and smiled. "That remains to be seen. Either way, would you at least think about my proposal?"

Andy thought of the loneliness he felt each time he stepped through the doors of his parents' house. Someday he might not feel that way. Someday it might make a good home for his own family. He smiled and thought of Estella's comment. It might make a good home with Mary Beth. But right now the gift Mrs. Nelson offered him was exactly what he needed.

"I'd like very much to move in with you. I'd like to know that there's someone waiting for me at the end of the day. Someone who loves me . . . someone I love."

Estella reached out to him. "Oh, Andy. Only God loves you more than I do."

Andy hugged her close. *Thank you, God.*

Thank you for the gift of this woman's friendship and love.

Estella pulled back and dabbed at her eyes. They stood in the cold night air, the darkness enveloping them like an embrace. "Look at the stars, Andy. So many—so crisp and clear—almost as if you could reach out and touch them."

"Like the stars you said the congregation put on the Christmas tree at church. It's like each one is a memorial to those who've sacrificed their lives," Andy murmured.

"What a wonderful thought, Andy. It is indeed like that," Estella replied. "And how appropriate. When Jesus came into this world, a star appeared in the skies in His honor."

Andy shook his head. "I'm not sure I understand."

Estella smiled. "Jesus came as the ultimate sacrifice for freedom. A star marked His arrival. The wise men went to find Him, led only by that star and God's hand. Now we look to the skies and remember those who've fought in this war—who've given their lives that others might live in peace and freedom. It just seems a special way to remember them and to remember what God has given us."

Andy put his arm around Mrs. Nelson and looked back up at the silent stars. No blue, no gold—just the wonder of God's handiwork and the precious reminder of His selfless love—a love that made life worth living.

AN INTRICATE WEAVING

of Mill Town Intrigue and Romance

I f you want more small town drama, join Tracie Peterson and
the talented novelist Judith Miller for their winning BELLS OF
LOWELL series. With list-topping sales, this is a series that has cap-
tured the hearts of readers everywhere.

Lowell, Massachusetts, at the end of the 19th century is a town
on the brink. Facing corruption, looming strikes, and lurking dan-
gers, this is a town where young women must be strong to survive.
Examining mill town life through the perspectives of three women,
the series brings readers all the romance, history, drama, excitement, and thrills they can handle!

Daughter of the Loom • A Fragile Design • These Tangled Threads

 BETHANYHOUSE